WOLF & WITCH

EE JUDD

RED SKY PRESS

1

———

Ruka stood across the street from a nightclub in the very early morning, inwardly debating yet again whether she should go inside or not. She blew out a puff of breath, watching it swirl and dissipate. The thought of being surrounded by a crowd of humans made her uneasy, and she check her magic reserves more for reassurance than necessity.

She used to be human too, once upon a time, but it had been so long since she had been among them that she felt awkward and conspicuous. She pulled out a pocket watch from her long skirt to see that it was one in the morning. Ruka had been waiting there for nearly an hour, and still her apprentice hadn't come out. She'd been patient, but enough was enough; it was time to take action.

Humans formed a line at the front entrance of the club, waiting for the bouncers to give them entrance, laughing, fighting, and flirting with one another. Their outfits were impractical, almost blinding with neon, ruffles, spandex and acid wash jeans, their hair puffed high and cemented into place with hairspray. Ruka almost viscerally recoiled at the thought of joining them in line. She'd use magic at the backdoor instead.

Her hand went to her waist before remembering she'd left her holster and bags at home. As an attractive woman with long blonde hair and floor-length full skirts, she already drew enough eyes among the almost blinding fashion of the late 80's, so she'd opted to come without her usual equipment.

Ruka reached into a large skirt pocket instead, drawing out a pinch of chamomile and ground moth wings. She whispered a short incantation, sprinkling the powder in front of her face, and felt the spell taking effect. Walking across the street, she veered around two drunken men who gave her a quick glance before ignoring her, the magic telling them she was nothing of note.

The alley behind the club smelled like garbage, urine, and vomit. Ruka tried not to wrinkle her nose at the stench. Humans were disgusting creatures; unable to deal with their daily misery, they choose to poison themselves until they acted no better than animals. Or worse.

Narrowing her eyes at a steel door dirty with grime and spray paint, Ruka retrieved an artifact from her pocket, a heavy key made of iron with runes etched deeply along the handle. She had charged the key earlier, so she only needed to place it on the knob, trigger the artifact with her power, and the door would unlock with ease.

Ruka nearly reeled back when she opened the door, instantly overwhelmed by the mind-numbing music. When she stepped inside, the stink of booze and moist, sticky air clung against her skin. The sooner she found her wayward apprentice, the sooner she could leave this place.

A hallway stretched out in front of her, dark and dingy. Ahead, Ruka could see a seething mass of bodies on the dance floor, strobe lights flashing in intervals completely at odds with the music. That was where she'd find Olivia.

She didn't want to be there. But her apprentice was only weeks away from her witch baptism, and the pressure had made the girl turn to risky outlets such as drinking every night and running around town with demis, getting into Goddess knew what kind of trouble.

Straightening her shoulders like she was getting ready for battle, Ruka made her way down the hall and into the throng of people, weaving around drunk and high humans who gyrated against each other, whooping and holding their hands in the air.

She scanned her surroundings, hoping to catch a glimpse of Olivia, but it was hard to see with so many people. Ruka wondered if she had any spells for such a situation, when she caught sight of long, frizzy red hair. The hair's owner turned in a circle, her head thrown back in laughter at something one of her companions said, and a shot of relief ran through Ruka. Thank the Goddess, this wouldn't take long then.

Squeezing around two dancers who were grinding their hips together, Ruka came up behind Olivia and tapped the redhead's shoulder. Olivia spun around with a curious face that froze when she saw who it was, and her smile melted down into the realization that she was in big trouble.

"Olly, who's this?" A girl wearing a blue puffy mini dress asked, hollering over the noise.

Two men, who were clearly with the girl and Olivia, squeezed in closer. Their eyes scanned Ruka with appreciation. A quick chant let her reach out her power and confirmed what she'd suspected: the girl and two boys were deminaturals, which meant the spell she'd cast didn't work on them.

"Is she a witch?" one of the boys asked, his expression dopey and stupid from too much alcohol. "Hey. Hey Olly, is she a witch?"

Olivia licked her lips, glancing between her friends and Ruka before giving a brief nod.

"Ooooh, mamma witch is hot!" the boy said. "Come dance with us!"

He tried grabbing Ruka, but she easily evaded his reach.

"It's time to go now, Olivia," Ruka said.

Her apprentice hesitated, then turned to her friends. "I gotta go," she slurred. "I'll call later, 'kay?"

The other boy, who had been silent until then, scowled and took Olivia by the wrist. "Wait," he said. "It's still early. Just tell her you don't wanna go."

Olivia looked torn and tried to free her arm, but the stupid boy wouldn't let go, his fingers squeezing and making her wince.

"Release her now, demi," Ruka commanded.

The boy scoffed. "Fuck you, bitch," he said. "You think you're so hot because you're a witch?"

Ruka's power rose and the boy's hair flickered yellow and orange, small flames rippling down his arms to Olivia's hand. The boy was definitely a deminatural, and one with a fire affinity.

"Ow! Rick, let go, you're hurting me," Olivia said, trying to pull free.

This was ridiculous. Ruka pressed her lips together and shot a bolt of raw magic at the boy. He gasped in a gulp of air and dropped to his knees on the sticky floor.

"What the hell," the girl in the blue dress screeched, crouching to check on her friend.

"Ruka!" Olivia said, sounding panicked. "Did you kill him?"

Ruka gave a sigh, feeing an enormous headache coming on. "Do you honestly think I'd kill a person over such a minor disagreement?" she said. "He's merely unconscious, and will wake up in a few minutes. Now, let's go."

Taking her apprentice under one arm, Ruka pushed through the crowd toward the entrance, past the hulking bouncers and into the open street. She drew in a deep breath, feeling lighter now that she was away from the noise, the stench, and incessant crush of humans.

"I'm sorry, Ruka," Olivia mumbled. "I know you told me not to — hold on, I gotta puke."

Ruka aimed Olivia to the gutter and held the girl's hair back while vomit splashed onto the asphalt. Olivia sputtered and coughed before straightening, one handing wiping her chin.

"I'm sorry, Ruka," Olivia said again, completely miserable.

"Come on," Ruka said. "Let's go home. We'll get you a remedy and a hot shower. Then, once you've sobered up, we'll talk."

Olivia sniffed. "Okay."

The drive home was quiet, with Ruka silently pondering the best way to deal with this.

Ruka had never wanted to take an apprentice – she'd worked hard and sacrificed so much to get where she was – but her dream was to become the next Witch Mother, and coven law dictated that candidates must have taught one or more apprentices. Over time, Ruka had become very fond of Olivia, and even realized she enjoyed teaching.

Olivia was talented, but her heart was too soft, and while Ruka appreciated her puppy-like affection, it made the girl practically incapable of saying 'no'. Which was a problem, because with her baptism coming up, Olivia could not afford to begin her supernatural life entangled with demis. It would ruin the girl.

Her hands clenched on the steering wheel. Ruka knew that mistakes and heartache were unavoidable, but she wanted to spare her apprentice the harsh struggle for respect and independence that Ruka experienced when she was a fresh witch.

Pulling the car onto the familiar street of her apartment, she slowed in front of a wrought-iron gate hedged by a high stone wall. A familiar tingle rustle over her as they approached the entrance; a protective rune that acknowledged its owner and automatically opened the gate.

"We're here," she said.

Olivia startled awake and blinked out at the familiar two-story building, ivy crawling up its stone walls. Ruka eased the car over the gravel drive, passing the lush gardens and lawns until she parked in front of the building.

"Go up and have a shower," Ruka told her. "Then come back down and I'll have a potion to get rid of the alcohol."

Olivia sighed but obeyed, trudging up the outside stairway to her apartment on the top floor.

RUKA RETREATED into her workroom and, surrounded by the aroma of herbs and secrets, began brewing. By the time Olivia stumbled in, the potion was ready and quickened with magic, and within minutes of drinking it, Olivia was back to her sober self, sitting on the sofa, fidgety and anxious, she waited for the inevitable scolding.

"Olivia," Ruka began, tucking her long skirts under her as she took a seat on the armchair. Her long blonde hair caught under her bottom, and she tugged it out with annoyance.

"Your baptism is only a few weeks away. You can't afford to be making mistakes now. I've seen other girls postpone cutting off ties with their human friends until the very last minute, and it never ends well. Do both them and yourself a favor, and begin distancing yourself now."

The girl burst into tears, and Ruka sighed, wondering if she was being too harsh. She hated feeling like the bad guy, but associating with other species only led to trouble, and demis were especially bad.

Demis were humans who mysteriously gained a magical affinity for anything from the elements to living things. Unlike species with long histories of self-governing and organization, they were a selfish bunch with no laws or rules they felt themselves holden to. They were nearly as wild as werewolves, and a dangerous influence on a young witch.

"Dry your tears, I'm not going to eat you," Ruka said, and Olivia wound down into sniffles.

"I just — I just thought that if I made some supernatural friends, we could still hang out after my baptism."

Ruka massaged her temples, reminding herself that Olivia was just young and struggling to adjust. She was young once, and the decision to give up her old life had been an easy one.

"I understand the transition is difficult," Ruka said, "but why demis? There must be a few other apprentices or even new witches your age to become friends with. What about that girl... what's her name? Wysteria's apprentice.... Veronica! What about her? She seems nice."

Olivia gave a red-eyed, scornful look. "Are you kidding? All she talks about is studying. She's a total nerd."

Ruka, known for her devotion to her lessons back in the day, resisted the urge to snap back defensively.

"I'm too old," Olivia continued. "All the other apprentices are younger than me and formed groups already. Can't I just keep one or two demi friends? Please?"

"Olivia, we've been over this. I understand you feel out of place and uncomfortable with the upcoming changes. But you're still able to contact your family, and once you're baptized, you'll make witch friends easily. One of the excellent things about witchcraft is that age no longer becomes an issue. It will get easier."

"Easy for you to say," Olivia grumbled. "You're gorgeous and talented."

"Flattery doesn't work on me," Ruka said with wry amusement, trying to provoke a smile from her apprentice.

It was true many considered her to be a beauty, and

although she was over forty, she still looked to be in her late-twenties. Although a witch's aging slowed from the constant use of magic (and a few choice spells and potions), eventually youth and beauty faded, leaving behind only talent. Olivia would understand that in time.

"Have you given more thought to your witch name?" Ruka said, wanting to change the subject.

Olivia straightened, eyes lighting up. "I narrowed it down to two names, but I can't decide."

"What are they?"

"Olive and Ginger. I really love those two."

Ruka struggled to keep a straight face. Good Goddess, the girl had poor taste. "I see. Why do you like them?"

"Well, Olive is close to my human name, like Ruka is close to yours. Ginger is cute because it matches my hair."

Witches should not influence their apprentices in deciding their witch name, Ruka reminded herself. It was part of the rite of adulthood, choosing a moniker for the rest of your life.

A witch's name was both an identity and a badge of honor, and upon their death, was engraved into the Great Tree of the coven hall's garden. To influence a witch in her choice of name was controlling. A witch belonged to no one but herself.

Still, perhaps she could sneak in just a hint or two.

"I chose the name 'Ruka' because it was similar to my human name. I won't go as far as saying I regret it, but sometimes I think I should have given it more thought," Ruka said. "When you become a witch, you must leave your human past behind. Humans don't understand what we do. They become jealous when they see our power and that we don't age. We do not exist to make their lives easier, we exist to keep the Balance, and that doesn't always go over well."

Olivia looked a little crestfallen, and Ruka patted the girl's hand.

"Don't fret too much. The moment you're baptized, you'll

know what your name will be. It could be one of those two, but it could end up being something completely different. No matter how hard you plan, sometimes life takes you by surprise."

"Do you ever miss it? Your human life, I mean?"

The question took Ruka by surprise.

Witches were essentially humans with great potential, with potent life force easily converted into magic after their baptism and training.

Witches scouted most girls from a young age and carefully watched over until they turned eighteen. The ones not selected as apprentices often became prominent people, their talent and ambition leading them to become leaders, innovators, and athletes.

Ruka's master took her in at fourteen, earlier than most. Her father had died in the war, and her mother drank herself to death, forcing Ruka to grow up quickly.

When her master approached her, she was more than happy to throw off the shackles of humanity to become something better, something great. She'd fought hard to learn and grow, and rose quickly as a powerful witch, one of the strongest in the coven and perhaps the region.

Even now, there were rumors that she was on track to become their coven's next Witch Mother, a great honor and responsibility. She would never risk that for nostalgia.

"No," she said, "I don't miss my human life. Transitioning from human to witch is like... seeing only in black and white, and then suddenly your world blossoms into color. Trust me. Once you gain the gift of magic, you won't care about past ties. Being a witch is superior to everything else; humans and demi friends included."

"That sounds lonely. Didn't you ever want to have a family? A husband maybe?"

Ruka suppressed a groan of exasperation. "Why would I be

lonely? I have my work, which is both satisfying and meaning-ful. I have a group of sisters who understand and support me, and I have the Mother, who watches over and protects us all. They are my family, and they will be yours too. We protect each other, and we protect the Balance; good and evil; life and death. If I had a husband or children, I would have to give much of that up. Although, there's nothing wrong with taking on a few lovers."

Olivia blushed and then sighed. "I can barely get guys to notice me, let alone become my lover. And the sisters are nice and all, but I don't like the Witch Mother much. She just seems so scary and calculating."

"Enough," Ruka said, more sharply than intended. "Don't talk about things you don't understand. Becoming a witch is a great blessing, but also a burden. The Mother has many responsibilities and works to keep our coven prosperous and safe. She can't afford to let emotion cloud her judgement or it may cause disaster or death. If you criticize her again, I'll delay your baptism for another year. Am I clear?"

Olivia hung her head. "Yes, Ruka," she said.

Satisfied the girl was sufficiently apologetic, Ruka got up and gave her apprentice a one-armed hug.

"I know you're struggling," she said. "I know, because I've been there too. But I promise — I promise — that it's going to be okay. I'll be with you the whole time, and for years after."

"Thank you," Olivia said.

She cleared her throat and Ruka released her, glad the evening ended on a pleasant note. It was so late it was early, the sky lightening from indigo to breathy pinks, and she was more than ready for bed.

The phone rang, making them both look up. Ruka left her apprentice at the table and went to answer it. "Yes?"

"Sister Ruka," a voice said, and Ruka immediately recognized it as Arwin, the Witch Mother's aid. "The Mother requires your presence in the coven hall."

"Very well," Ruka said. "Should I prepare anything?"

"You don't need to bring anything, but..." Arwin's voice became jittery. "You should know that Hunters are here."

A ball of anger and anxiety formed in her stomach. "I see. I'll be there immediately."

2

The coven's headquarters was an old courthouse three stories high, with elegant windows, stone pillars, and a bell tower. Back in the fifties when the city hit a boom, they decided that the old stone building was an outdated relic, and embraced the times by moving their government into a modern hall with glass exterior walls and ugly beige brick.

The coven had a different Witch Mother back then, and she was savvy enough to smell an opportunity. She swooped in to buy the old building, and, with a tempting pot of coven funds and a bit of magic, the deal was done. Thirty years later the city realized its mistake and tried to get the building back, but if there was one thing you should never do, it's mess with a witch.

Now, as Ruka strode up the cobbled path lined by expansive gardens and the coven's magnificent Great Tree, she felt a sense of pride for all her coven had achieved together. Witches came and went, but the hall, the Coven, and everything they stood for was timeless, a fact that gave Ruka comfort.

Inside the marble-tiled foyer, Arwin paced while waiting. The witch hurried to meet Ruka, her pristine white skirts brushing the floor, hair braided neatly into a coil around her head.

"Ruka," Arwin said, looking relieved. "Thank you for coming. They're in the main hall."

"How long have the Hunters been here?" Ruka asked, following Arwin up the grand stairway and toward closed double doors.

"I called you soon after the Witch Mother granted them an audience. That was thirty, maybe forty minutes ago."

"I wish there was a spell to clear traffic," Ruka muttered, annoyed by the delay. She couldn't think why the devious Hunters were here. Perhaps, having destroyed covens in other cities recently, they were here to threaten the Mother. Her lips tightened, determined to make them pay if that were the case. "Do you know what they want?"

"Our help, apparently."

Ruka stopped and stared. "What?"

The aid shrugged, biting her lower lip. "I didn't hear all of it. The Mother and Dusk are in there now."

Ruka straightened her dress and muttered a quick spell to smooth her hair. Then, raising a fist, she knocked three times.

"Enter," came the Mother's voice.

Arwin flashed Ruka an encouraging smile as the doors swung open of their own accord, and Ruka walked into the audience chamber, head high and hands folded neatly in front of her.

The main hall was the building's largest room, elegant with a domed ceiling, wood-paneled walls, and a massive fireplace to one side. Originally designed to accommodate sizable crowds for federal or high-profile court hearings, it now served as a celebration and ritual hall for the coven, and an audience chamber for guests. Or in this case, enemies.

She eyed the four Hunters who sat along a long table facing the front, looking uncomfortable in their gray and black uniforms. Whoever designed their clothing was clearly trying to replicate some sort of futuristic military outfit, but the effect only made them appear ridiculous and hot.

At the front of the chamber, the Witch Mother sat on her chair. To the left of her stood Dusk, one of the most ancient crones in the coven and known to be fairly neutral in coven politics.

The place to the Mother's right was conspicuously empty.

"Your daughter gives her greetings," Ruka said, cupping both palms and touching her forehead. "I have answered your call."

The Mother gave a benevolent smile. "Welcome, daughter."

Official greetings done, the Mother gestured to the empty spot beside her and Ruka strode smoothly to take her place, staring down her nose at the Hunter delegation.

"This is Ruka, our finest witch. She'll be the one to investigate this so-called necromancer."

Ruka forced herself to keep a calm, even expression, but inwardly reeled. She hadn't a clue what the Mother was talking about and was shocked she was being volunteered without discussion first. It wasn't like the Mother to breech etiquette, so Ruka held her tongue, trusting there was a good reason.

One Hunter, the only one standing, inspected Ruka with a judging eye. "She looks young."

"I'm not," Ruka replied tartly. She shouldn't let his comment get under her skin, but she was already tired and on edge. She realized she looked young, but appearances meant nothing to witches.

The leader arched an eyebrow. "Uh huh. Look, we need someone with practical experience, not just a pretty face. This guy is dangerous."

"I am not a mascot, Hunter," Ruka retorted. "All the witches in our Coven are strong and competent." She smiled politely with cold eyes. "I'm dubious you can say the same about your little... organization."

Several of the Hunters' faces darkened at the insult, but their leader just looked amused.

"Ruka is our best," the Mother said calmly. "She will get the job done."

The Hunter leader stared at her a moment, his fingers tapping on the table, then he shrugged. "Okay. I'll have my people drop by in an hour with the case file. All the info you need is in it. We look forward to seeing results."

They stood, sending wary glances at the three witches. Their leader gave a polite smile that Ruka didn't trust for a minute, then they all hustled out as if they had somewhere important to be.

The door closed behind them, and Ruka turned to the Mother with annoyance. "What exactly am I supposed to be doing for them?"

The Witch Mother smiled. "Do you resent me for volunteering you without your consent?"

She did, but she wouldn't admit it.

"No, Mother," she said, bowing her head slightly. "I understand you must have had good reason to do so, but I feel uncomfortable with this situation. A Hunter asking for a favor is... unusual."

Arwin came in, hurrying to help the Mother stand.

"It is unusual. But also a rare opportunity. Walk with me for a while," the Mother said, waving away Dusk and Arwin.

The coven's leader tucked her hand into Ruka's arm, and the two strode unhurried out of the main hall's back door, their soft shoes tapping against thick wood plank flooring. The Mother was quiet for a while, lost in thought, and Ruka waited patiently until they came to the records library. They wandered past rows of shelving stuffed with ancient tomes and took a seat on a thick bench under a window, motioning for Ruka to sit beside her.

"In the last year," the Witch Mother finally said, "the Hunter organization has raided and destroyed two covens, as you know. The last raid took place only three months ago."

Ruka nodded. "Yes, of course. They killed so many of our sisters," she said, anger and sorrow gripping her throat.

"Yes. It was a significant loss for our kind. So much knowledge destroyed. All because the Hunters covet our power." The Mother's face pinched in fury. "Their wanton destruction has taken a toll on all witches. If we were to go to war with them, I'm uncertain we would win."

"They cannot be that powerful, surely! They're only humans."

"Don't underestimate humans. We have strength, but they have numbers. The Hunters are no longer the vigilante group we once knew them to be, hiding in caves and cellars, making homemade silver bullets in basement forges, and antique equipment. They've made an agreement with the human government and received resources to become a serious threat."

Ruka scowled. "It's not enough for them to only hunt dangerous renegades. They keep wanting more, and more, and more."

The Mother nodded grimly. "Humans are like a disease, gobbling up and destroying everything they can. Only *we* follow the will of the Goddess and do what we can to protect the earth from their greed."

Ruka knew the Witch Mother could go on for weeks about her disgust of the humans, but they were getting off topic. "What is it they want from us then?"

"They want us to find a necromancer for them."

Ruka blinked. "Surely they don't need our help for some undead-loving warlock."

The Mother chortled. "It's true. Apparently, this necromancer has been using unusual magic, and they're not quite sure what to do with it. They can't even find the man."

"So I'm to track down this necromancer, and then what?"

"That's it," the Mother said. "You simply need to track him down."

Ruka gaped. What a ridiculous use of her skill set!

"I can see you're not pleased by this."

The Mother was looking at her now with an unreadable expression.

"I have some concerns," she admitted. "If the task is only to find a rogue necromancer, why not send one of the others, like Benadere or Meadow? I have a lot of work to do, and my apprentice's baptism is only a month away."

"I understand your hesitation, but your involvement is necessary."

"And why is that?"

The old witch cracked a smile, and Ruka saw hints of her craftiness. "Because using someone of your caliber puts them further into our debt. If I send another witch - a lesser witch - they could argue that the reward I ask for is too much. I will allow them no such argument."

"And what reward will you ask for?" she asked, impressed by the Mother's craftiness.

With a mutter, the Witch Mother waved her hand and Ruka felt a trickle of power as a book eased out from its place on a nearby shelf, coming to rest heavily in the old woman's hands. Wrinkled hands turned the pages without hesitation until they came cross the passage she was looking for.

Her brows drawn together, Ruka leaned over to read and after the first paragraphs looked up at her coven leader sharply. "A treaty?"

"We had them in the past," the Mother said, tapping on the yellowed, crinkly paper. "Long ago, after a devastating war between our kinds, the Hunters and the witches came to an agreement: for fifty years, there would be a cease-fire. Each group would leave the other alone, a blessing that would allow each side to rebuild their strength and numbers. They eventually broke the ceasefire, of course, but the witches had twenty years of peace, and could regain enough strength to resist the Hunters ever since."

"Will they really agree to such a thing for simply tracking down a necromancer?"

The Mother closed the book. "Well, our treaty won't be on the same scale. The deal will extend only to our coven, and for just five years. Five years is a lot of time, however, if used properly."

It was a lot of time. Ruka thought of the names carved into the coven's tree in the last five years. So many sisters lost. Bright sparks of wisdom and magic — destroyed by the Hunters.

"Can we perhaps lessen the time period and include our sister covens as well?"

The Mother gave her a penetrating stare, and Ruka suspected she was being evaluated. "Our own Coven's welfare is our priority. I cannot sacrifice the safety of the sisters under my direct care for worldwide goodwill, no matter how much I wish it."

Seeing the expression on Ruka's face, she added, "Rest assured, I'll convene with the other Mothers and discuss how they might benefit from this as well. If the Hunters can't even find the 'undead-lover' as you call him, they may have trouble taking him down as well. In that case, I'll refer them to our sister covens so they may also gain leverage."

It was a good plan. Ruka's coven could gain amnesty simply by popping out and casting a search spell. Then, by referring the Hunters to other covens to help with the more dangerous job of capturing, they would increase goodwill with the other covens without risking the lives of their own. Ruka felt unsettled by the idea of putting her fellow witches - even though they weren't in her coven - at risk, but the Mother was right. They had to protect themselves first.

"I see what you mean," Ruka said thoughtfully. "Very well, I'll do as you ask."

"Excellent. I'll send Arwin to deliver the documents. In the meantime, I suggest you spend some time talking to that apprentice of yours. I hear the silly girl is involved with demis."

3

Ruka peered out her car's windshield at a farm, eerily still in the misty moonlight. She wished she arrived during daylight, but it took the Hunters hours to send the documents, and then it took her several more hours to drive to the location.

When she'd gotten the documents, she learned why they had come to the witches for help: a whole Hunter team had gone missing without a trace. Ruka could handle herself, but she still felt uneasy in her gut and wished she had asked for one of her sisters to come along.

Well, she was here now. She double-checked the array of pouches and potions on her hip harness. It should be enough for anything a necromancer threw at her.

The earth was damp under her feet when she got out of the car. A barn sat near the road, red paint flaking and a roof sagging with rot. Further into the property, Ruka made out an old farmhouse, two stories with a wrap-around front porch. Old trees surrounded it, and Ruka saw a rope swing hanging from the branches of one.

Both the house and the barn were dark, but for good

measure, Ruka pulled a pinch of comfrey mixed with ground salt from a pouch at her waist, and threw it into the air while muttering a quick chant. Magic rolled out like ripples in a pond, the echoes returning to tell her what she already suspected: there was nothing alive here.

She checked the barn first, placing her feet carefully and wrinkling her nose against the stale moldy straw and feces. She also set up a shield around herself, though she was certain the necromancer was long gone.

A strange energy prickled against her senses, sliding just above her skin like a balloon charged with static. Ruka was familiar with most types of magic, including those from other supernatural species, but this was new.

Curiosity peaked, she wandered inside the barn, focused on finding the source.

When the Hunters claimed there was a magic they couldn't identify she'd thought they were just incompetent, but it seemed they were telling the truth. The magic felt bitter and foul, but it was unique, and Ruka's scholar soul fluttered in excitement at the thought of discovering something new.

If only she could pinpoint it.

The strange energy flicked on and off, like the movement of a clock. Even more frustrating was the source seemed to come from all around the barn, and every time she thought she figured out where it was coming from, it would 'tick' from a completely new position.

Disgruntled, she rolled up her sleeves and was about to clear a spot to sit for spell casting when headlights illuminated the gravel road outside the barn door. An engine rumbled to a stop near her car, and the engine turned off.

Perhaps it was a friend or relative coming to check after not hearing from the family for several days. Or it could be Hunters. Neither were welcome, so she'd have to chase them off.

Ruka took a moment to cast a second magical shield and crept back to the entrance.

She put her shoulder against the barn wall and peered around the opening, but saw only the outline of a truck parked next to hers. Taking a pinch of eyebright and chalk from another pouch, she cast a vision spell. Her eyes burned for a moment and then she could see as clearly as if it were day.

No one was in the car.

Sighing at the expenditure, Ruka took another pinch of salt and comfrey and threw it into the air. She muttered the chant under her breath and wheeled back with a gasp as the spell identified something just around the corner of the barn.

A shadow sped around the corner and leapt straight for her. Ruka threw up a hand and threw a shot of raw, sizzling magic from her palm.

The man twisted midair and landed ten feet in front of her, crouched with hands and feet on the ground. His eyes reflected red and gold, a snarl curling up the corners of his mouth to reveal sharp fangs.

Her eyes widened and she stumbled back, hastily double-checking her shield. Of all the things she thought she would encounter, a werewolf was outside her realm of expectation.

"Are you the one who took my Packmate?" he said in an aggressive tone, the words garbled through a mouthful of teeth.

"I beg your pardon?" Ruka asked, confused.

He growled and took a threatening step toward her. "I said, are you the one who took my Packmate?"

"I have no idea what you're talking about," Ruka said pertly, shaken but determined not to stand down, "You shouldn't be here, though. It's dangerous."

The werewolf cocked his head, violence draining from his posture. "You're telling the truth."

"Of course I'm telling the truth."

What on earth was a werewolf doing here? Before Ruka

could put the thought into words, a strong tick of magic fluttered against her skin and her attention snapped to the back of the barn.

"You should leave now," she whispered. "Something is coming."

The wolf man lifted his nose to the air and, rising to his feet, stared into the depths of the barn.

"Dead flesh," he said, and the hair rose on Ruka's arms.

If she was dealing with a necromancer, that meant only one thing.

She strode back inside. The wolf jogged up beside her, and she suppressed her irritation. The idiot was going to get himself killed.

"Do you even know what we're up against, wolf?" she asked.

His only response was to growl again.

"It's a necromancer," she told him, straining to roll the barn door open wider. "He likely left an undead slave behind to see who showed up. Are you able to handle an undead?"

"Crafty bastard," the werewolf said, ignoring the question and shoving the door with ease. He shook out his arms, readying himself. "On guard, witchy woman. It's coming."

The corpse clawed up from under the dirt between two stalls. Necromancers used their power to reanimate dead bodies that would mindlessly carry out any command they gave and also used magic to hide their servants in shallow graves.

That must have been what she felt before: the spell in a sort of hibernation mode, waiting to meet certain conditions before exposing and animating the undead. Then again, she hadn't sensed the thing when she was in the barn, only pinpoints of magic outside. Some array she wasn't familiar with? Perhaps the necromancer set up a spell that would wake the undead if over one person breached it. Or perhaps it had been waiting for a werewolf.

The corpse was only a couple days old and stumbled toward them on awkward limbs, its milky eyes rolling. At least it was the slow kind. She wasn't fond of necromancy in the first place, but weak, lower undead were much easier to deal with than higher servants. Those ones were strong, fast and sometimes intelligent.

"Stay back," Ruka warned the werewolf.

Ignoring her instruction, he skulked forward, the muscles in his back tense.

Ruka gritted her teeth. She quickly gathered a large portion of raw power and threw it forward ahead of the werewolf, blowing the zombie to bits. It was an inefficient and brutish use of magic, but satisfying.

Chunks of flesh flew through the air. An arm hit the ground in front of her, bouncing to land on her boot, but that was the only piece that reached her. The werewolf, however, had raised his mutated hand to strike, and instead of hitting the solid creature, got a face full of rancid blood and half-rotted meat that now clung to him in sticky globs.

He froze, looking down at himself in horror.

"What the hell was that for?" he asked, and she bit her lip when a clump of intestine on his scruffy brown hair flopped as he spun around.

"I beg your pardon, but I did tell you to stay back."

"I heard you, and I thought you were being patronizing again," he said, trying to wipe the mess off his face and spitting in disgust when it got in his mouth. He sounded exasperated, but not angry, thank the Goddess.

Ruka couldn't help the huff of amusement that escaped. "Perhaps I was a bit hasty," she said.

The wolf looked up as if properly noticing her for the first time. He scanned her from the boot toes that peeked out from under her skirt, up to the top of her blond head, then chuckled, black-brown old blood oozing a trail down the left side of his face. "Well, don't worry. I admire a woman who can take quick action."

And then he flat out winked at her.

Ruka felt her mind stutter to a halt. Was he... flirting with her?

Now that he wasn't angry and snarling, his features stood out better. Warm eyes crinkled above an arched nose, and his mouth turned up at the corners like a mischievous imp. His brown hair desperately needed a cut, though it was hard to tell under the spray of exploded entrails. If he cleaned himself up and shaved, he'd probably be handsome in an all-American kind of way.

"What are you doing here, anyway?" Ruka asked.

His smile faded.

"One of my pack mates had family here. When they went missing about a week ago, he got permission to come visit, and now he is missing. I'm here to find out what happened and bring him back home."

Privately, Ruka thought that the Packmate probably got himself killed by the missing group of Hunters. And come to think of it, what was this werewolf doing out alone when one of his Pack had already gone missing? It seemed like a risk, but who was she to judge werewolf behavior?

"Well, as long as you don't interfere with my work, feel free to look around," she said. It was time to get out of the barn. Not only did it smell like dung, but now a rotten meat smell was trying to crawl up her nose.

The werewolf joined her outside. "Actually, why are you here? A few minutes ago you mentioned a necromancer. Care to share information? I've never collaborated with a witch before."

Ruka lifted her chin. "I have no obligation to share anything with you. We'll each investigate on our own, then you go your way and I go mine."

"But what if it's dangerous?" he asked, looking worried. "What if I get in trouble and need you to save me?"

She pressed her lips together, unsure if he was mocking her. He seemed uncharacteristically easygoing, so he wasn't likely a dominant wolf, but she doubted his Pack would have sent a submissive out here alone, so she estimated he was a middleweight. He likely could take care of himself.

"I'm sure you'll be fine."

His face split into a grin and, now that his eyes weren't glowing, she noticed they were a honey brown. He wasn't exactly handsome, but something about him caught her attention. Werewolves generally had an extra something about them, but this one in particular had an intelligent look in his eyes that caught her attention; though it could just have been the fact that his entire head and torso was caked in blood.

"Ya, that's true," he said, "But if you get into a fix, just call and I'll come running."

How silly. She didn't need the help of a coarse werewolf. "Thank you, but that won't be necessary."

"Well, you never know." He shrugged and made his way toward the house. "Oh! I didn't introduce myself. I'm—"

"Good Goddess, Wolf," Ruka snapped, finally losing patience. "I don't need to know your name! Please go away, you're distracting me."

He heaved a pathetic sigh and left, hands shoved despondently into his pockets. Once Ruka was satisfied he wouldn't come back, she got to work.

HER GOAL WAS to create a rune that would fully sample and analyze the area's residual energies, but also create a vision of what happened when the mysterious magic was first used. It was an advanced spell, but doable for someone of her caliber.

Taking the largest pouch off her hip harness, she studied the gravel area just outside the barn and once she found a spot she liked, began drawing the rune.

It was a complex design, and the wood ash mixed with ground human bone was precious so she took her time, working carefully to not waste a single bit or make any mistakes.

The entire rune took ten minutes to finish, and Ruka stepped back to critique her work. She'd made a circle about ten feet across, its perfect shape a testament to decades spent honing her craft. A second circle lay just inside the first, and between the two she'd drawn the symbols needed to define the spell's purpose.

In the very center was a third, smaller circle just large enough for her to sit inside, and six lines divided the entire rune into six portions. In the outer pie pieces, Ruka placed tokens she drew from yet another pouch: stones representing earth, air, fire and water, and a piece of polished bone and dried umbilical cord in the remaining two that represented life and death.

The rune would suck in magic within thirty meters, sort it by element, and channel it into the center where Ruka would sit with an artifact. The artifact would store a portion of the energies in exact percentages and patterns for a full analysis later.

In normal circumstances, she could match the magical signature against all known necromancers that the witch collective knew of, past and present. Considering how bizarre and alien it felt, Ruka doubted whether she would find a match.

She'd still be able to study the magic later and determine what made it so different. There were also several witches both in her own coven and other covens who loved to study unique powers, and she could split the signature stored in her artifact three times: one to study herself then store in the coven's archives, and two more to offer for outside analysis.

Ruka stepped into the third circle, placing her artifact dead center. She used a small amount of magic infused just enough into the rune to set it. Now that there was no chance of scuffing the lines, she sat confidently with the artifact in her lap, and cleared her mind.

The power came when she called, filling her body and hovering until she spoke her spell, it flowed out from her, into the circle. She provided the magic, but the symbols she'd drawn on the outside would organize it, and increase efficiency and potency.

The last symbol filled, and the rune hummed with power, gathering, sorting, shifting and magic into place like a magnet making passes over iron filings.

She observed with anticipation as the rune drew in all energies in the area, shifting through the residue. The artifact in her lap just started sucking it in when she heard the first moan.

Ruka held perfectly still, hoping she'd just imagined it. But when another moan came, this time from a different direction, her heart sank into a pit in her stomach.

Two corpses stumbled around each side of the barn, and she drew in a sharp breath when four more followed. Including the one from earlier, that made seven undead, which was ridiculous. Most necromancers could only keep five to seven corpses animated at a time. Had he left all his servants there?

The first two undead crossed the outer ring of her rune. Ruka could smell their sickly sweet decay, and with her night vision showed ugly, gaping wounds on their faces and bodies. The closest one wore a white robe of some sort, with dark brown splotches Ruka instantly recognized as dried blood. It raised its arms and brought them down on her head.

The sound and odor of sizzling flesh hit Ruka all at once and she flinched, bile rising in her throat. The corpse flew through the air, landing in a motionless heap ten feet away. It didn't rise again.

But the second undead had arrived, and the four others twenty feet behind.

A drop of sweat trickled its way down Ruka's temple. She couldn't halt her spell now. To do so would not only waste the magic she'd already spent, but the backlash would leave her weak and nauseous and she wouldn't be able to cast spells again for several days. It was better than being eaten, however.

The second undead lunged for her and the shield threw it back as well, but Ruka's outer shield flickered and died. She watched nervously as the undead's arm twitched. But though it wasn't fully dead, the magic had damaged it too much to get back up.

Two were down, but four undead still came for her, shambling with hungry moans that made Ruka's heart beat faster. She had one more shield, but even if it could destroy undead three and four, she'd still be undefended against the last two.

A shiver ran through her at the thought of their hands clawing at her clothes and hair, their sharp teeth tearing at her skin. The image of Wolf came to mind. He'd hear if she called for him.

But the thought of relying on a werewolf to save her raked her pride. Her innermost shield was stronger than the outer one, and might hold against the remaining four undead. Yes, she decided, she'd trust in her shields.

Another bead of perspiration trailed down the side of her head and tickled her cheek. The rune was nearly done. But as the third undead reached for her, Ruka wished desperately that there was some way to hurry the spell. She cursed herself for making such a complex rune when a simpler one would have done. She wouldn't be able to analyze it if she were dead, and she really, really did not want to die.

Ruka watched as undead three and four attacked her one

after another, and died permanent deaths. The shield held, but flickered weakly, and Ruka wasn't confident it was strong enough to destroy undead numbers five and six.

She had to decide, and quickly. Should she cancel the rune spell and try to escape to the safety of her car? The undead were strong, but they weren't quick, and even if she were weak as a kitten she could probably make it.

Undead number five tripped and fell face-first onto the ground a few feet in front of her. Thank the Goddess that magic locked the rune's ingredients in place until the spell completed, because the disgusting thing raised its bloated face and pulled itself along the ground with bloody arms. Ruka's leg twitched, the urge to kick out at the thing almost overwhelming. The spell teetered, and she sucked in a panicked breath, focusing before it snapped and stunned her.

Now both undead were six feet away. She was out of time.

Her hands felt clammy. If she was going to stop the spell and leave, she had to do it now. Should she stay? Should she run for it?

Just as she decided the only way to survive was to risk the backlash, something flashed in and landed behind the undead.

Wolf snarled, wicked sharp claws held out threateningly. He darted forward, swinging a fist with dizzying speed, and the head of the first undead collapsed inward, ichor spattering to the ground. He made quick work of the last undead, and after scanning to make sure there were no more, returned to her.

Gone was the teasing, easygoing expression. He looked as wild and angry as when she first saw him, and Ruka wondered if she'd just exchanged one danger for another.

"What are you doing?" he demanded, eyes pure yellow. "I knew witches had their heads in the clouds, but to think you would just sit there while six zombies tried to eat you is pure stupidity."

He was scolding her, Ruka realized numbly. Her shoulders

slumped and her hands started shaking, the reality now hitting her about just how close she'd come to death. She wanted to answer him, to give some pithy response that would sooth her fear and wounded pride, but the spell tugged at her, demanding attention as it came to a climax.

Wolf stood there glaring like a disapproving father. If he wasn't about to attack her, then she could safely ignore him for the moment. She tuned out his voice and neatly closing off her spell, unfolding her legs with a groan of relief.

"Thank you for your assistance," she said, "but I had it under control."

He looked at her with disbelief. "You know I can smell lies, right?"

Her cheeks burned, but the rune bursting into light saved Ruka. Wolf scrambled backwards until he wasn't standing in it.

"What's happening?" he asked.

His eyes were brown again, so his little tantrum must be over. Ruka pocketed the artifact containing the precious magical signatures and finally got up.

"Turn around," she said.

Giving her a mistrustful look, he did, and yelped.

Behind him stood two misty figures. Wolf slashed at the closest, leaping backward as if expecting retaliation, but the figures didn't acknowledge his attack, or even his presence.

"Don't bother," Ruka told him, feeling vindicated. "It's a vision spell, one that will show me exactly what happened when the necromancer first cast his magic. Since you were kind enough to provide assistance - unasked for, I'll remind you - I'll allow you to stay and watch."

Wolf gave her a look, then sighed. "All right," he said. "I accept. So what happens now?"

"Wait a moment. The spell is still forming. It should begin—"

She broke off when the two wispy figures moved.

One was clearly an undead, so the other had to be the necromancer. A dark cloak covered him from head to toe, and he was about six feet tall compared to her own five foot eight frame. Just barely taller than Wolf.

The apparitions went straight for the house, and after exchanging a grim look with Wolf, Ruka followed.

4

———

The necromancer headed straight for the house where the family would have likely been asleep. Stopping twenty feet away, he raised a pale, distorted hand. He sketched something in the air, a notoriously difficult type of rune-casting that had gone extinct. Who was this man?

"What's he doing?" Wolf whispered in her ear, causing Ruka to jump.

"You don't need to be quiet," she said at normal volume. "It's an apparition. They can't hear us."

"Right. I knew that." He looked embarrassed.

"As for what he's doing... he's casting some sort of spell on the house. A silence spell? No, there's no reason for him to wait outside for that. His casting is unique," she said, tapping her lower lip with a finger. "I wonder who his master was."

Another minute passed as the necromancer just watched the house. While they waited, Ruka tried to peer up inside the necromancer's cloak but it was like pure darkness covered his face, rebuffing all light.

"Is something supposed to happen?" Wolf asked, shifting impatiently.

"I don't — wait, someone is coming out of the house."

Movement at the front door drew their attention. The farmer came out first, his wife trailing numbly behind, both still in their pajamas. They didn't act afraid, or nervous, but plodded along as if asleep.

The couple came right up in front of the necromancer and stopped, their faces blank. Ruka studied them, frowning at the looks of stupor.

"These are the relatives of my Pack member," Wolf said. Then he growled.

Looking up, Ruka's stomach clenched as four children exited the house, one after another.

"What is he going to do with the kids?" Wolf asked, pacing.

"I don't know," she replied. "But it can't be good. Most necromancers have at least the decency to leave children alone - their corpses are too small and weak to make good servants - but there are a few spells that require the blood of virgins, or young children. Those spells are forbidden to all witches and warlocks."

Again, Ruka wondered who had taught this man. Or perhaps he'd simply found hidden books or scrolls that taught ancient necromancy. Regardless, she'd report this to the Witch Mother, and leave it up to her. If they left capture of the necromancer to the Hunters, this information would at least be helpful in preventing deaths.

The children lined up next to their parents. The necromancer walked down the line, his head tilting and bobbing like a bird as he inspected them. In particular, he seemed taken with the youngest child, a boy with messy blonde hair, dressed in a t-shirt and shorts. He was five at most.

Inspection done, the necromancer stepped back and waved at his servant. The undead attacked the husband, reaching with putrid arms to gather him toward itself. It sunk ragged teeth into the warm neck, thick fluid running down the man's chest and shoulder.

The man's legs buckled, but the undead followed him to the ground and kept savaging until the necromancer snapped his fingers. Like an obedient dog, it let go of its prize and dove for the legs of the wife, ripping flesh from one of her thighs.

Ruka shivered as awareness bloomed in the woman's eyes. The woman shed a tear but couldn't move her muscles enough to outright cry. The necromancer crouched down and pushed his face up to the wound, watching as his servant moved up to her hip.

Ruka's stomach turned. A quick glance at Wolf showed his eyes were glowing again, his breath strained, and she remembered that these people were family members of his Packmate. Perhaps he'd even known them.

If there was any consolation, it was that the vision couldn't reproduce sound. If it could, Ruka didn't know if she'd be able to stay if she heard the wet sounds of teeth ripping flesh, or the woman's whimpers.

Finally, the woman couldn't support herself anymore and fell to the ground beside her husband. The necromancer stood and waited as his undead servant ripped her throat as well.

Once her body stopped moving and her eyes glazed over, he pulled a knife from his belt and made a nick in one finger.

He pressed the finger to the foreheads of both husband and wife, and now Ruka wished that that spell had sound so she could hear what he was chanting. She patted the artifact in her skirt pocket, making sure it was still there.

"What's he doing now?" Wolf asked.

"Raising the bodies," Ruka said. "He's extremely talented. No wonder the Hunter team disappeared."

"Hunters?" Wolf said. His face took on a wary, predatory look. "How are Hunters involved?"

Ruka held up a hand. "Later," she said. "Something is happening."

The bodies on the ground twitched and jerked for several seconds, then went still. When they moved again, it was in the slow, fumbling way of true undead.

The necromancer waved his hand, and two spots on the ground shivered open. The farmer and his wife occupied each grave, curling up and letting the earth cover them until they disappeared. Only a slight mound remained, easily missed unless you knew what to look for.

"They weren't buried when I came to the house," Wolf said. "I found pieces of them in the field behind. I think that Denver - my Packmate - had to fight them. Poor kid. They raised him, you know. His mom was a human, and she dumped him with his aunt here when he was three. The wife is his biological aunt. I can't imagine having to fight the zombies of your family."

"You said you found the remnants of these two," Ruka said. "Did you find your Packmate's body as well?"

He shook his head. "Maybe he ran off, but if that were the case, he would have contacted us."

"Perhaps he went wolf-mad. I hear it can happen in extreme circumstances."

Wolf crossed his arms. "Doubtful," he said. "We would have heard something from the nearest village, or at least the other farms in the area."

"Hmm," Ruka said, not fully convinced.

This wasn't the time to debate, however, because the necromancer headed for the barn, the four children in tow.

"Now what?" Wolf asked, and he and Ruka trailed along behind.

At the barn, the necromancer waved his hand, and six misty forms stepped from the road onto the farm's property.

The necromancer took his entourage around the outside of

the barn, stopping six times to cast the magic that would bury and hide his servants in the earth where they'd be safe until someone sprung the trap. That done, he left the children at the door and stepped inside the barn with the last servant, which he also buried.

"This man has an impressive amount of magic," Ruka murmured with a shiver. "He would be a formidable foe for most."

"But not for you?" Wolf asked.

Ruka scoffed but didn't elaborate when he raised an eyebrow.

Outside, the necromancer beckoned toward the oldest of the four children, still under thrall. The boy looked about eighteen years of age, and he walked right up to the necromancer until they were so close they were almost touching.

Reaching up, the necromancer removed his hood, and Ruka gasped.

"What?" Wolf asked. "What is it?"

She waved at him to be silent, unable to take her eyes off the figure in front of her.

The necromancer was bald, with papery skin that clung to his bones. His ears were shriveled, the tips crumpled into gnarled points. What disturbed her the most, though, were his pure black eyes.

Ruka had seen sketches in ancient texts that closely resembled this so-called necromancer. It shouldn't be possible, though. The last one had been killed over five hundred years ago.

And yet as she watched, the man - no, the creature - opened its mouth to reveal fangs even longer than Wolf's. It leaned into the boy like a lover and plunged its teeth into his neck.

Wolf leapt backwards, growling and snarling like a wild thing.

"What is that thing?" he asked, eyes locked on the two figures.

The thrall spell had broken the instant teeth broke skin, and the boy shuddered and thrashed in the creature's grip.

He yelled silently, his eyes rolling in panic. Slowly, his hands stopped beating at the head clamped to his neck, his eyelids drooped. The boy's eyes stared off into nothing, but positioned as she was, Ruka felt like he was looking right through her.

She watched with a tight chest as the light left his eyes, and the body dropped to the ground, drained of blood.

"That *thing*," she said, finally answering Wolf's question, "is a vampire."

"Vampires don't exist," he said immediately. "They haven't existed for centuries."

"And yet..." She gestured to indicate the creature in front of them, licking the remnants of blood that had smeared around its mouth.

The vampire performed the same rite as before to raise the body of the teenage boy. The boy picked up the smallest child, and followed the vampire and two other children back to the road, disappearing from the spell's range.

"This changes everything," Ruka said, a chill reaching her bones. "Let's go sit in my car. I don't feel like having a conversation here."

Obediently, Wolf followed her back and took a seat in the passenger side.

Ruka steadied herself, calming the whirl of thoughts and emotions that were a mess inside her head. Wolf waited with fidgety hands, and once she was ready, told him everything she knew: how the Hunters contacting the witches for help, and how the Mother chose her to analyze the magic left behind.

"So you won't find him and kill him?" Wolf asked, more calm than she expected.

"The Mother told me I was to analyze and do no more. However, that was when we expected just a rogue necromancer. This is way beyond my expectations. Beyond anyone's expectations."

She felt a little better about being saved earlier. Obviously, a simple necromancer wouldn't have been able to leave so many undead behind, so she hadn't actually been unprepared, merely misinformed.

"Now that we know it's a vampire, I want to do more."

Wolf straightened. "You'll hunt it down then? I still haven't found my Pack member, so you can count on me for backup."

Ruka gave him a scornful look. "That would be foolish," she said. "Vampires are incredibly strong. It would take more than just you and I to kill one."

"I'll locate its nest tonight and leave the cleanup for the Hunters. If they request our help again, it will be up to the Mother to decide what to do."

Wolf looked like he ate something rotten. "You'd leave something like this to the Hunters? I don't trust them."

"I don't trust a werewolf I met an hour ago either."

This time he looked offended. "I'll have you know I'm very reliable."

"Reliable or not, there's no way the two of us could fight against a vampire. It's also not wise for me to act before consulting the Mother."

"Do you always have to ask your Mother before acting?"

Ruka's hands itched to pull his ear like she would a naughty apprentice. "Don't you need to ask your Alpha before taking action on something like this?"

He paused. "Ah. Well... yes. So you mentioned locating its nest?" he said, changing the subject.

"Yes. Even if we can't kill it tonight, I'll feel a lot better at least knowing where it is."

"Good. Let's do that then," Wolf said.

Ruka stared out the windshield at the spot where the vampire had killed the boy. That's where the vampire's magical signature would be strongest, but her mind revolted at the thought of sitting there.

Banishing such weak thoughts, Ruka forced herself to leave the car. It was best to just get this over with so she could go home and report her findings.

SHE STRODE with brisk steps to the spot, gingerly scraping gravel with the toe of her boot. A week had gone by since the family was reported missing, and it had rained since then. Perhaps it was cowardly of her, but Ruka felt relief that no blood had remained.

She quickly set up two barriers, and remembering the last fiasco, cast a third. It was a lot of magic, but she had enough in reserve to perform the tracing spell and defend herself.

She was almost certain the vampire had left no more servants behind, and just as certain that Wolf meant no harm. But the close call had shaken her. It was better to be safe than sorry.

Examining the pouches on her waist, Ruka selected a small one containing ground fluorite, an excellent choice for discernment. She dumped it into the mixture of bone and ash.

"Let's get started," she said, and formed the rune.

It was more complicated than the one she'd drawn earlier. Although that one had blended two functions into one - magic analysis and the spell of seeing - the effects themselves were straightforward. This time, however, she knew she was dealing with a very crafty, ancient creature, and there were too many unknowns to take chances.

She included every safeguard she could.

"What does this one do?" Wolf asked. His genuine curiosity

combined with the fact that he was staying out of her way made Ruka generous.

"This will prevent the vampire from taking control of my spell."

"Huh. And this?"

Ruka followed his finger to another symbol. "That will prevent him from tracing it back to me."

"So it won't know where the spell is coming from?"

"It can still pinpoint the location where it was cast, but I don't want it latching its filthy magic onto me and tracing me back to my coven or home."

"Right," Wolf said. "That would be bad."

She snorted. "'Bad' is an understatement," she said, recalling several horrific descriptions from her books of vampires that attacked Covens.

She continued to explain every symbol she drew: one prevented magical back flow (the vampire could flood his own power into the spell, forcing it backwards and overloading her); another prevented it from flat out stealing her magic and storing it for itself. She fed the signature she'd collected into the rune to specify her target.

Ruka hesitated when it came time to choose the actual tracking symbols. There were many methods to track someone with magic, and she needed one she could share with others since she doubted the Hunters would simply take her word for it. She chose a mapping symbol and placed a glass marble on it, and in a last-minute decision, added a divination symbol.

"What's this for?" Wolf asked.

"The magic enters the marble. I can place it on a map later, and it will roll to the vampire's location."

He looked doubtful. "Doesn't sound very accurate."

"It depends on the size of the map. But you're right, on its own it wouldn't be helpful, which is why I also added this divination symbol. Many witches prefer using a live compass symbol, but in this case that's risky."

"Oh?" Wolf asked, studying the two symbols. "Why is that?"

Ruka held up a finger like she was giving Oliva a lesson. "Because it creates a semi-permanent link between the witch and the target. If I were tracking a human it would not matter, but a vampire..." She shivered. "I'd prefer not linking myself to the thing in any way. Now, no further questions. It will take me some time to finish drawing everything. I'm going overboard, but better to be safe than sorry."

It took Ruka half an hour to get everything drawn. By the time she finished it was nearly dawn, the sky blushing gold and purple. The perfect time to do the tracing spell, Ruka thought with satisfaction, since the vampire should have gone to sleep.

"That should do it," she said, standing and stretching her back.

"Massage?" Wolf offered, holding up his gore-covered hands.

She gave him a dirty look. "Kindly keep your paws to yourself."

He shrugged, not even phased by her insulting tone.

"Suit yourself," he said, and smirked when she sat with a wince.

"Stay out of the circle," she told him.

"I'm not in it."

"I know that, I'm simply telling you to — You know what? Stop talking, I need to concentrate."

Again he smirked, and she wanted to smack it right off his face.

The fit of temper was unlike her, and Ruka made herself take deep breaths to clear her mind. She couldn't afford to make a mistake just because he unsettled her.

Once she steadied herself, Ruka opened the channel inside her and welcomed the magic, carefully feeding it into the rune.

The complexity would take a lot out of her, leaving her reserves dangerously low.

The power rushed through her, greedily latching onto the symbols she'd drawn. The power made her feel giddy and light-headed. It had been a while since she'd used so much magic in a single day.

Outside the circle, Wolf paced back and forth, likely disturbed by the magic and uneasy with nothing to do.

Finally, enough power filled the rune. Sweat beaded and itched on Ruka's brow. She felt weak and shaky. There was still more to do, however, so she gritted her teeth and forced herself to hold the connection in place and check every symbol, ensuring the power distributed perfectly.

Once satisfied everything was in place, Ruka closed the connection to the rune and stiffened as it flashed with light. Wolf covered his eyes with an arm.

Ruka's perspective blurred and shifted. When it cleared, she was looking at the interior of an old church.

The vision flickered and blurred at the edges. There wasn't much time.

She was at the front of the church, and could see that someone had removed the pulpit. In its place was a coffin, and the spell told Ruka very clearly that her target was inside.

The vision wouldn't allow her to physically move, but it gave her sight and sound, and she noted everything she could. The church seemed to be small, only one level, but with a tall, vaulted ceiling.

On the organ she could make out a songbook with printing on the cover. Property of Rosedale Anglican Church. That was helpful.

A scuffing sound caught her attention, and her eyes snapped back to the coffin. The lid opened gradually and white, desiccated fingers eased out from the inside.

Ruka reeled back, ending the vision early.

When she came to, Wolf was holding her, his eyes boring into hers with anxious concern.

"Witch," he asked. "Are you okay? One minute you were fine, and then you just lost consciousness. What happened?"

"I'm fine. Get off me," Ruka said, trying to move him away. She might as well have tried moving the barn.

Wolf gave her some space, but still gripped her arms. "Are you sure? You were pretty out of it."

"Of course I was," she said with a huff. "It was a vision, part of the spell."

"You know, that information would have been nice to learn beforehand."

This time she freed herself and stood on wobbly legs. "If you'll excuse me, I'd like to get out of here before the vampire sends a servant to investigate."

"Unless zombies can drive, it'll be awhile," Wolf said. "And you're avoiding the issue. I was worried when you just keeled over all of a sudden."

The genuine concern in his voice took Ruka aback, but then anger rushed through her.

"You need to understand something," she told him. "We aren't friends. We aren't allies. I didn't ask for your help and don't expect it. I've been doing this for many, many years, and don't need a werewolf to lecture me on how to take care of myself."

"Oh, my mistake," he said, eyebrows raising dramatically. "I didn't realize that almost getting killed by zombies and going unconscious during your own spells was taking care of yourself. No doubt your many, *many* years of experience renders you invulnerable."

"Don't take that tone with me, Wolf," she told him. "I'm well over forty years old, and not some young pup you can boss around."

"Forty! My God, that makes you practically *ancient*," he said, and this time she couldn't let his sarcasm go unchecked.

"Well, I'm sure that must be young to such an old, powerful werewolf such as yourself," she said, acid sizzling on every word.

"Pretty much," Wolf replied. "I'm 82."

Her brain stuttered to a stop.

"Hell-spawned werewolves," she muttered, turning her back to hide the deep flush that heated her cheeks. She clenched her fists and began marching back to her car.

"That would be 'old' hell-spawned werewolves," Wolf said, easily keeping up with her.

She glared at him, lips pressed. "You're really enjoying yourself, aren't you?"

"Well actually, I—"

A heavy, sharp tang burned at Ruka's supernatural sense, and in unison, their heads snapped back to the barn. Ruka's eyes widened to see a spark of light flicker in midair. It snapped and crackled with power, then widened until it was like a massive glass pane that distorted the farm fields behind.

Through it, undead poured out.

5

—————

"Holy moly, how many are there?" Wolf asked, his eyes wide.

"A portal," Ruka said, trembling in awe. "It can make a portal. How?"

"Not the biggest concern right now, witchy woman."

The first of the zombies had locked onto them and shambled over. Behind them, undead continued stumbling out of the transparent, rippling surface until nearly two dozen had gathered. The portal shivered and shut itself.

"It is a problem," Ruka said, eyeing the horde with trepidation. "If he can make a portal anywhere, then nowhere is safe. Not my coven, not your Pack territory."

Wolf shrugged his shoulders and Ruka heard them pop as they shifted to reinforce themselves.

"One thing at a time," he said, his words muddled. "Let's take care of these first."

He launched himself forward, plowing through the first three undead like a wrecking ball. They made juicy noises when they hit the ground, but immediately moved to get up again.

Ruka's hands moved to her waist. Her left hand pulled out a blade twelve inches long, and her right, a pinch of sulphur from her holster. She threw the powder into the air, and as it floated to the ground, she chanted a hasty spell. Magic infused the sulphur and flames burst from her fingertips, engulfing all three of the undead struggling to get to their feet.

The flames were so hot they were blue and clung to the undead, who rapidly shriveled into blackened husks and stopped moving. Next, Ruka grabbed a small vial of energy potion from her belt and ripped the stopper out with her teeth. It tasted like muddy weed water, but the rush of energy felt like the world's strongest coffee, a much-needed boost for her exhausted state of mind and body.

Not far off, Wolf grabbed the head of an undead and ripped it off, jerking loose from the grip of three others who clawed hungrily at his clothes. He danced on the edge of the horde like a wild beast, eyes glowing and claws hurling chunks of flesh and congealed blood into the air. Undeterred, the undead clawed and scratched for him, their jaws working as if eager to sink their teeth in to his flesh.

Ruka took a breath and launched herself to join him, plunging her dagger into the eye of the one undead her flames hadn't fully destroyed. It sunk in deep before hitting the back of the skull, and Ruka struggled to free the lodged blade with mounting urgency.

Something gripped her blouse from behind and she spun, slamming raw energy into the rotting face of the creature. It flew backward, knocking into another. She finally worked the dagger free and threw herself at them, ramming the blade over and over into their eyes and temples until they no longer struggled to get up.

Her hands and face were wet and felt sticky, and Ruka gagged a few times before steadying herself. She wiped the gore off her face with her sleeve and looked around.

Nine undead were on the ground, not moving, but there were still twelve left.

Wolf was doing an incredible job of leading them in a wide circle, darting in and out of the horde to deal what damage he could. But although werewolves were fast and strong, undead were relentless. They didn't feel pain and never tired, so it was just a matter of time before they overwhelmed him.

Ruka focused inward and checked on her magic reserves. The previous spells had cost her, and while the potion only energized the body, it couldn't restore her power.

Her legs cramped when she stood. Several undead notice the movement and broke off from the primary group to head for her. For a moment, she wondered if she should run while the werewolf had most of the horde's attention.

No, she couldn't do that. She didn't know how much she could help, but Ruka was no coward.

Pulling a healthy pinch of powdered clay from a pouch, she held it to her forehead and whispered a quick incantation, monitoring the two undead who were only fifteen feet from her.

Wolf was doing well - better than she thought - but sweat was matting his hair to his forehead, and multiple lines of fresh blood traced his skin from scratches and bites, though his werewolf magic had already closed the wounds.

Ruka threw the charged powder to the ground, commanding the earth to soften. The undead slowed, sinking ankle-deep into the dirt, and some toppled right over. It wouldn't hold forever, but it hopefully bought enough time to finish killing them. It had to, because she was out of magic.

Black spots played at the edge of her vision, and the horizon tilted dangerously.

Wolf was already taking advantage of the trap and twisted off three heads in succession, the snap of bones and tearing of flesh causing bile to rise in Ruka's throat. She swallowed it down and put one heavy foot in front of the other, facing down the two undead six feet away.

Wolf growled.

"Stay back," he called. "I'll come kill those, just get some distance."

She ignored him and leaned back to avoid the rotted, grasping hands.

"Worry about yourself," she retorted.

Taking a firm grip on her knife, she let the closest undead grab her, using its own strength to push the knife up into the soft palate of its mouth. Goddess, the things smelled horrific. She'd burn these clothes once she got home.

The undead stopped struggling, and Ruka pulled the knife free but overbalanced, nearly fell onto her backside. The second undead seemed to grin at her, its jaw working as if it was already imaging her tender flesh between its teeth.

"Just run, dammit!" Wolf called again, sounding frustrated.

She heard cloth ripping and then something heavy and wet splat onto the ground.

"Just hold on, witchy, I'm almost there!"

There were six undead still stuck in the earth spell, but Wolf abandoned them to come help her. He snagged the back of the undead's white coat and jerked it backward with enough force to part the thing's arm from its body. Wolf looked at the limb with surprise before tossing it aside and held out a hand to help Ruka up.

She batted his arm away. "Leave me be," she said, "Your hands are disgusting."

He blinked at her.

"Okay then," he said, and spun to punch an undead who had worked itself free from the earth and snuck up behind him. Its nose crunched, and it fell to the ground, where Wolf immediately stomped on it with heavy force. Only four remained.

"There we go," he said. "You're welcome, Witch."

"I didn't ask for your help," she said through gritted teeth.

"Oh? Well, I'm sorry if I got in the way of you and a horrible death."

Ruka's cheeks burned with anger and humiliation at being saved - again - by a werewolf. Furious, she fumbled for a health potion and downed it, the aches disappeared and some strength returned.

Now that there were only three undead left, Wolf sauntered over and grabbed one by the back of the neck. It fell forward, landing on its knees, and Wolf twisted to keep his grip, digging his claws in deep until they came out the other side, curling his fingers around its spine.

One of the other two undead worked itself free, and Ruka scrambled to her feet, dagger in hand as the thing grabbed Wolf's hair. He yelped and leaped into the air like a startled cat, but his hand was still embedded in the first one's neck. His eyes widened in surprise and he landed onto his side with an 'oomph'.

"Do you need help?" Ruka said sweetly, hysterical laughter threatening to bubble up inside her at the sight of an undead gripping a werewolf by the hair.

"No, I'm — ow! I'm fine," he said, finally getting free. He patted his head and glared at the undead who still clutched a clump of sandy brown hair.

"You little shit," he growled.

In a move almost faster than Ruka's tired eyes could track, Wolf darted forward and hamstrung the undead, slamming his knuckles into the skull of the other who was still ankle-deep in dirt. It reeled but didn't go down.

Ruka stepped forward with her dagger to help, but before she could get close enough, Wolf raced behind and grabbed her by the back of her waistband. The air heaved out of her as he jerked her backward, and she fell onto her backside.

One last jab with his claws killed the last undead, and silence descended over the farm again.

Wolf crouched in front of her, close enough that she could see every brilliant fleck of gold in his eyes. "Are you okay? I told you I had it," he said, sounding exasperated. "You don't need to be reckless."

"And I told you I didn't ask for your help," Ruka said, pulling her shirt from him. She started to re-tuck it, but seeing how filthy it was, left it. "Do you make it a habit to manhandle women? Kindly step back so I can get up."

His eyes narrowed, but he relented and stood up, giving her space. "You are, without a doubt, the craziest woman I've ever met."

Ruka shrugged. Not her problem.

"I like it!" he said. "I like it a lot."

She gaped at him.

He grinned, which looked disturbing with all the blood and gore that spattered his face. Were all werewolves this odd? Admittedly, she hadn't talked to many, but she'd always gotten the impression they were more... animalistic and brooding. Wolf seemed more like a kid despite his old age - which still rankled her - and his easygoing manner kept throwing her off.

She rummaged a clean handkerchief from inside her blouse and rubbed her face. Her hand shook from the aftereffects of adrenaline and the potion.

Looking around, she frowned when she noticed something. "Are those Hunters?"

Wolf dropped the dopey grin and studied the body nearest him.

"It looks like a few of them are," he said, sounding serious again. "Six of them, looks like."

"Wonderful," Ruka said. "I think I know what happened to the missing team. If I had to guess, the vampire set a trap for them too, and it didn't go well for the humans."

Something else occurred to her. "Your Packmate. He isn't here, is he?"

Wolf shook his head. "No. I don't know whether to be relieved or more worried. He could have escaped, or he might be dead - or undead - somewhere."

He looked distraught, and Ruka felt a twinge of sympathy. If it were one of her sisters who went missing, she'd be eager to know what happened to them.

Thinking of her sisters reminded her she needed to get back and report what she'd found. She was eager to analyze the magic, and the marble for the map spell was burning a hole in her pocket.

"I need to go home," she said, pushing herself onto her feet with a groan. "The Hunters will come by to clean up this mess, so don't worry about staying."

Wolf offered a hand, but she rejected it. He followed her back to the cars, hovering with ready hands in case her legs gave out. Which was an embarrassing possibility.

Once she was safely behind the steering wheel, she sighed in relief.

Wolf put a hand on the hood and stared down at her through the open window. "Would you like me to escort you home?"

"Unnecessary," she said automatically. In reality, she wished someone would drive her home, but her pride wouldn't allow her to show this werewolf any more weaknesses.

"Stubborn," he murmured.

He stepped back when Ruka turned the ignition, and the engine roared to life.

"Well. It's been fun, werewolf, but this is where we part ways."

"For now, Witchy," he agreed. "My Packmate is still missing, so our paths might cross again."

It was time to leave. Ruka put her car into gear, already

looking forward to a hot bath. Her headlights swept across the scene of carnage as she turned around, but the image that stuck in her mind the most was of Wolf walking back to his truck, covered head to toe in brownish-red gore.

In the rearview mirror, she saw him raise a hand in farewell, that mischievous grin on his face.

He was trouble, and she was glad to see the last of him.

"You want me to work with werewolves?" Ruka asked, struggling to keep her composure.

It had been a full 24 hours since she'd gotten back to the city and reported to the Mother. Afterward, she'd rested and meditated for most of the day to recover before tackling the magical signatures she'd gotten at the farm.

Unfortunately, this had proven fruitless. Nothing she tried let her identify the magic the vampire used, and as a result she was frustrated by the time the Mother called her to report.

The Witch Mother calmly turned pages of an ancient tome without looking up. "Not just werewolves, you'll be working with the Hunters as well."

"I — what? Why would you agree to such a thing? You said we would leave the capture to the Hunters and other covens. Am I expected to follow the orders of humans and dogs? Not only that, but once again you included me without my permission."

The Mother looked up now, her eyes sharp and lips pressed together. "It's your own fault, girl! I told you to identify only, but you had to do a trace spell, didn't you? You were to leave it alone, but instead you escalated the situation."

Ruka paced. "As if I could leave it alone! It's a vampire. A vampire! Goddess, the thing could stalk us and kill our coven members one by one."

"Yes, thanks to you drawing its attention," the Mother said.

"It was only a matter of time!" Ruka insisted. "The farm is only two hours away from here, and at such a close distance, it will discover us eventually. I thought it was best to gather information to place us in a stronger position. I thought you would have approved."

She slammed the book shut and her voice took on a waspish tone. "No matter how clever you thought you were, you disobeyed me and put our coven in danger. The instant you cast that spell, the vampire would have known witches were nearby, which would have taken longer if you hadn't poked your nose in."

Ruka's temper flared. The way the Mother worded it put her on edge. Ruka had been the one to do most of the work, and it was her life on the line. The Mother was treating her like a servant, and not a free witch in charge of her own choices and destiny.

In all likelihood, the vampire already knew of them and was simply biding time to grow stronger. But the Mother's face was dark as a thundercloud, so Ruka forced herself to regain her composure, no matter how unfair it was.

The Mother sighed. "Daughter, you're talented, there's no doubt about it. But you need to look at the larger picture. It would have been smarter to bow out and let the Hunters track it down. By tracing the thing, you not only alerted it to our presence, but now the Hunters have decided you're indispensable. I cannot turn down their request for your assistance without losing the goodwill I've already built. You won't risk the lives of all our coven members just because I accepted the Hunter's request for help, would you?"

Ruka felt guilty. This wasn't the Mother's fault. It was true Ruka had gone against her advice and perhaps acted rashly. There were many things the Mother knew that she did not, and no doubt had taken many actions that Ruka was unaware of.

Ruka's actions likely had disturbed carefully laid plans, leaving the Mother to scramble to recover.

Truthfully, she felt a desire to help hunt the vampire the moment she saw the children at the farmhouse. It was simply that they had given her no choice that was getting under her skin.

"I apologize," she said, calming herself. "In the heat of the moment, I made a judgement call. Whether or not it was correct, I will of course take responsibility for my actions."

Even if it meant dealing with Hunters and werewolves. Her eye twitched.

"Good," the Mother said. She tapped her fingers and sighed. "Oh, don't look so martyred, daughter. I won't send you in alone. You may pick four sisters to accompany you."

Ruka did some swift thinking. "In that case, I'll take Arabella, Wysteria, Dusk and Nine."

"Arabella to help with offence, Wysteria and Dusk for defensive spells. Why Nine? She is younger and less skilled than the others."

"Yes, Nine is less advanced, but she has a good head on her shoulders. She won't rise to the Hunter's provocation, and I've noticed during past emergencies she's the quickest to respond."

"True. Well, if those are the sisters you want, then I'll give my approval. I leave it to you to give them the news, but you may ask in my name. This is not much help, I realize, but I can promise I will reward you accordingly."

Ruka felt a twinge of irritation. Although she could use the Mother's name when asking the witches to join her, it carried less weight than an official directive, which was harder to refuse since it meant the coven was in danger. Even with the weight of the Mother's name, they would be reluctant to help hunt a vampire, let alone mingle with Hunters or werewolves.

It also meant that Ruka would be personally responsible for paying the sisters for their help, and there was very little the

Mother could offer to compensate for that. Ruka would suffer a loss.

"As you wish," she said, frustrated but unwilling to lose her status as the Mother's most dependable witch. "If that's all, I need to make preparations."

"Wait," the Mother said.

Ruka paused with her hands halfway to her forehead.

"Ruka," the Mother said. "Make sure you take the lead on this expedition."

"Oh? I had thought to make the Hunters and werewolves do most of the dangerous work."

The Mother waved a hand. "They're expendable, yes. However, we can't allow them to take credit for the success of this mission. I had hoped to avoid being in this situation, but now that we're here, we must take hold of the opportunity."

"You're saying that if we play a pivotal role, we'll have more leverage in treaty negotiations."

"You catch on quickly," the Mother said with approval. "The wolves have wormed their way into this mess for the same reasons, so you can't allow them to take all the glory. Our coven must gain the upper hand. Our survival depends on it. Can I count on you?"

Ruka cupped her hands to her head and bowed. "You can, Mother."

"Good. If you succeed, I will reward you by officially naming you as the Witch Daughter."

Her previous resentment dissipated and a thrill of excitement fluttered in Ruka's chest. This was her greatest wish! To be named the Witch Daughter meant the Coven officially recognized her as a candidate to become the next Witch Mother. The title went to only two or three excellent witches, and the Mother had been hinting for years she was close to choosing, but hadn't named a singled witch. Until now.

"Thank you, Mother. I assure you I will do everything in my

power to help the coven." She bowed deeply, her heart beating rapidly in her chest.

The Mother chuckled. "Yes, I thought that might light a fire under you. I'll let you make your preparations now. You leave at first light."

Ruka visited each of her chosen witches in person. As expected, they were reluctant about going on such a dangerous mission, and became sour when they learned Hunters and werewolves would accompany them.

In the end, she had to promise rare ingredients to Arabella, Wysteria and Dusk. Nine, who was only a few decades into her life as a witch, wanted to learn two spells that Ruka had personally developed.

Once negotiations were complete, she phoned Olivia and told the girl to come help finish preparations. She'd have her apprentice help make potions and magically infused snacks, and gather and check all the gear she'd need.

"You're fighting zombies?" Olivia said with wide eyes once Ruka assigned her tasks. "Holy cow."

"They're called undead servants, or just undead. Why is everyone calling them zombies?" Ruka replied, her mind going back to Wolf. Just the thought of him made her embarrassed all over again. She wished he hadn't seen her fumble so much that night.

"Um, all the movies call them zombies, you know? 'Undead servants' is kind of uncool."

Ruka's glare made Olivia flush.

"So, what will you need to fight these undead," the girl asked.

"Full rig," Ruka said.

Olivia looked shocked. The girl had helped her prepare for missions many times over the last two years of her apprenticeship, but Ruka had never fully kitted up during that time.

"Full rig?" Olivia asked with a delighted gasp.

Checking her list again, Ruka nodded. "Left and right belts, and both bandoliers. I was caught by surprise last time, but it won't happen again."

"You were caught by surprise?"

Her apprentice was getting on her nerves.

"Are you a parrot? Yes, I was caught by surprise. A good witch knows when to admit she made a mistake. The important thing is to acknowledge and correct that mistake. I underestimated my opponent on my last mission, however on this one I'll go in fully prepared."

Olivia hopped gleefully off her stool and ran for the glass cabinet where Ruka kept the weapons and tools she used on missions. "The long dagger or the sword?" she asked.

"The dagger," Ruka replied.

"What potions will you take?"

Thinking back to the previous fight, Ruka knew she'd need something to recover stamina and accelerate magic regeneration. She wouldn't need any poisons or antidotes for fighting undead, but health potions were always a wise choice. She'd also bring a few precious stones infused with as much power as she could stuff inside and drain in case of an emergency.

Olivia rummaged through her apothecary drawers and brought the ingredients and artifacts she requested. They spent the rest of the evening brewing, cooking and, in Olivia's case, oiling leather.

Finally, once Ruka was sure she had everything she'd need, she filled every hip pouch and bandolier slot she could, and tried on the whole ensemble.

It was a bit heavier than she'd like, but her plan was to use the Hunters and werewolves as guards while the witches cast spells from the back.

She stepped to the full-length mirror by her front door. The bandoliers crisscrossed her chest, their leather tabs stuffed with test tube potions and the few artifacts. The dagger hung in an underarm holster, in easy reach.

On her hips, two thick leather belts crossed each other. Various pouches clipped onto rings, adding enough bulk to look like an 18th-century bum roll.

She made sure she could move properly while Olivia looked on with admiration and envy.

"That should do," Ruka said, and let Olivia help her take everything off again.

"Will you need anything else?" her apprentice asked politely, fidgeting, and looked far too relieved when Ruka dismissed her for the evening.

She laid out her clothes for the next morning, then sat down to meditate and gather magic.

With a vampire, undead, Hunters and werewolves, she'd need every bit of power she could get.

6

———

"Do you have any good cassette tapes?" Dusk asked. The oldest witch among them, Dusk leaned forward from the back seat until she was practically breathing down Ruka's neck.

"There are some in the glove box," Ruka said.

Arabella, who sat in the passenger seat, shuffled through the collection.

"It's all pop music," she said. "I didn't realize you enjoyed that sort of thing."

"My apprentice gave them to me," Ruka replied.

"And you kept them?"

It had been a long two hours trapped in the same car with four of her sisters, and they were getting on each other's nerves. Sensing Arabella was baiting her about the music, Ruka felt palpable relief when a voice from the back interrupted.

"We're here," Wysteria said, rolling down the window and leaning out for a better view.

Ruka slowed the car as a sign that read 'Welcome to Rosedale' came into view. Just behind the sign, four vehicles lined up along the shoulder of the highway, and figures stood in two groups.

"Oh my. It looks like the circus is in town," Arabella said in a slow, scathing drawl. She eyed the group of werewolves, easily recognizable by their sloppy loose clothes and scruffy hair.

"We're getting along today, Arabella," Ruka said. "You can provoke them on your own time, but for the duration of this mission, we can't afford infighting."

A sneer marred Arabella's sharp beauty, but she agreed to Ruka's relief. Arabella was a powerful witch, but when she was stubborn about something, nothing could change her mind.

Dusk cackled, a huge grin on her wrinkled face. "Not a worry, sister Ruka, I'm in no hurry to give up the Luck Gathering Flower you promised. I can't wait to see Sissy's expression when I tell her it's mine."

In the rearview mirror, Ruka saw Nine, the youngest of them and who was sandwiched by Dusk and Wysteria, roll her eyes before returning her expression to neutral.

The Witch Mother held all rewards Ruka promised in escrow, and none of her companions would receive a thing until they returned. Ruka knew that despite their views on outsiders, each witch would do her utmost to ensure the mission was a success.

Wysteria, a witch with a deceptively demure appearance, leaned forward to get a better look through the windshield. "Well, well, who is this then?"

Ruka squinted out the window and groaned. "Wonderful," she grumbled. She tucked her keys into a pouch on her waist and got out of the car.

"Told you I'd see you around," Wolf said, grinning with delight as he stopped in front of her.

"Yes, hello again."

"Ruka, you know this... gentleman?" Wysteria purred.

Wolf looked at Wysteria with amusement and tilted his head so that his hair flopped into his eyes. "So your name is Ruka," he said, flat-out ignoring the other witch. "It doesn't suit you."

"I didn't ask for your opinion," Ruka told him, and scowled when he chuckled.

"As feisty as ever," he said.

She'd thought this before, but Wolf did not act like a proper werewolf should. He might just be an odd person, but she had the uncomfortable suspicion he was acting this way because he fancied her, and she didn't know what to do with that.

Wysteria and Nine were observing the exchange with interest, so Ruka let the comment go. If Wolf's interest became a problem, she'd just have to find a way to deal with it.

Another werewolf came up behind Wolf, and the two had a silent werewolf conversation that involved only body language and magic.

"Let me introduce my people," Wolf said.

Ruka raised her eyebrows, taken aback. "You're the leader?"

"For this mission I am," he said, ducking his head and looking shyly up at her through his bangs.

"Enough with the false humility, I'm not buying it," Ruka said.

Wolf burst out laughing. "Can't fool you," he said, and waved the rest of the wolves over.

All of them were men, and all of them looked like the hyper-masculine vagrants she expected from werewolves. Arabella and Dusk sniffed, but Wysteria blushed like a maiden. Nine gave no reaction.

"Denver, Benny, Porkchop and Harris," Wolf said, putting his hand on each on as he introduce them.

Denver was the only female werewolf there, and she gave a polite, uninterested nod to Ruka and the other witches.

Benny was probably as young as he looked, and his eyes

opened a little wider when he got a good look at her. Ruka was used to men finding her attractive, so did her best to ignore it, especially since Wysteria was eyeing him like he was a tasty piece of meat. The kid kept glancing between Ruka and Wysteria, pink-faced.

Porkchop suited his name perfectly, a meaty, roundish kind of man, which was impressive considering how difficult it was for a werewolf to get fat. His face held a congenial smile, betrayed by a predatory look in his eyes.

The last werewolf, Harris, bore a striking resemblance to Wolf, and had the same brown hair and eyes and the same plain face. But while Wolf's intelligent expression and constant mischievous smile made him seem handsome, Harris was somber and his eyes held shadows.

"This is Arabella, Wysteria, Dusk, and Nine," Ruka said.

"Feel free to call me Wystie," Wysteria said, "since Wysteria can be difficult to remember."

"How is it difficult to remember?" the kid Benny asked. "It's a flower. Why do witches always think everyone else is stupid?"

Dusk bristled and flicked her white braid over her shoulder, but Wysteria giggled. Arabella, already bored with the conversation, drifted back to the car.

A short growl from Wolf made Benny duck his head and shut up.

"I suppose you have a point," Wysteria said to the young werewolf. "Fell free to call me whatever you like then." She placed a hand lightly on his arm, and he glowered at her but didn't pull away.

Goddess help them all. Ruka was fully aware of Wysteria's healthy interest in the opposite sex, but this was not the time to add another man to her harem.

"Should we meet the Hunters, Ruka?" Nine asked in a soft voice.

"Yes, I suppose we should," Ruka said. She eyed the third group, the Hunters.

Their presence on this mission was non-negotiable, unfortunately, so she needed to work with them. That didn't mean she trusted them, however. Far from it. Aside from the bloody history between Hunters and supernaturals, she already felt a sense of distaste seeing this Hunter group's cocky bravado.

While the Hunter organization had gotten powerful sponsors and cleaned up over the past decade, they still carried a stench of wannabe syndrome, like they were doing their best to emulate how they thought proper soldiers would act. Only two men stood apart; one, a fit-looking blond with a crew cut, looked professional and focused on checking his gear and weapons. The second walked among the others, exchanging words and clapping them on the backs.

The remaining four Hunters horsed around and whispered what were surely rude remarks as they sized up the supernaturals. In Ruka's eyes, they were little more than glorified mercenaries.

Hopefully, they'd pull themselves together by the time they faced danger, but Ruka would keep an eye out for incompetence, malicious intent, or both.

She sighed, then approached them with Wolf glued to her side. The Hunters turned as they approached, the men staring first at her chest, then her face with appreciative smirks. Wolf edged forward slightly and crossed his arms, but Ruka stepped up to stand level beside him again, not needing the protective gesture.

"Are you Captain Huck?" Ruka asked the man who seemed in charge.

Ruka had the feeling she'd seen him somewhere before, and then realized he looked like the Hulk Hogan. He wore a bandana tied over long, greying blond hair, and an eye-catching white handlebar moustache that moved when he gave her a polite smile that didn't' reach his steel-gray eyes. "Yep, I'm Captain Huck, ma'am."

"Good," Ruka said. "I'd like you and your team to meet my sisters."

Another round of introductions began. Ruka introduced her witches, and Wolf introduced his werewolves.

On the Hunter side, Captain Huck introduced Wilson and Ed, who were the team's scouts. They'd go ahead of the group to check for danger, and report back. Ed was the youngest of the Hunters, with bulging muscles and a mullet. He made no effort to hide his distaste for supernaturals. Despite his antagonistic attitude, Ruka had the feeling the young man was all bark and no bite.

Wilson was a wiry, sharp man in his late thirties or early forties, with dark greasy hair and deep-set eyes that studied Ruka and her witches with a calculating expression. He reminded Ruka of a snake curled up in the grass, ready to strike. She put him high on her list of Hunters to watch out for.

Doug was a Hunter similar to Porkchop in appearance. He was short and heavyset, with a round, flat face and easygoing expression. While Porkchop's eyes burned with intense alertness, however, Doug seemed a little dumb. As far as she could tell, though, he didn't harbor hatred for her and the witches, so Ruka categorized him as a lesser threat.

The next Hunter, Archie, was probably the strangest of the bunch. He had greying hair and grey eyes in a rough, leathery face, and Ruka couldn't tell if his pleasant demeanor was an act or not. After Captain Huck introduced him, Archie proudly introduced the two gleaming revolvers strapped to each leg, Betty and Veronica. He named them after characters from his favorite comic, which his parents had named him after.

Finally, Huck introduced the last man, the crew-cut blonde

Ruka had noticed before who was the fittest and most professional looking of the bunch. Stan -- or Stan the Man as Huck said, clapping the Hunter on the shoulder with a wide grin -- gave a brief nod and a polite, "Sir, ma'am," to Ruka and Wolf, holding his rifled in an easy grip that suggested familiarity.

"This guy was in the Marines for a while, but one day his squad came across some enemy forces who turned out to be trolls. The Marine squad survived thanks to this guy here. After, he found the Hunters and joined us. And we're happy to have him, too," Huck said, beaming proudly like he was the man's father.

Stan, kept a blank expression through the whole story, giving Ruka no idea of his opinion of her or the other supernaturals. He didn't make her skin crawl, but he was clearly more skilled than the others so Ruka categorized him as a medium threat. At the very least, she would keep an eye out for disturbing behavior.

"Okay, so now that we've all met each other, let's get this tea party started," Huck said. "I don't know how many people in town the sucker's killed so far, but we're going in as quiet as we can so we don't attract attention. No cars, no magic."

Ruka watched with amusement as he began a long-winded explanation of formations and hand signals, explaining how they would 'clear' the town until they found where the vampire was hiding.

"That sounds all very impressive, Captain," Ruka said, "but we already know where the vampire's base is. Perhaps your superiors didn't mention it, but I narrowed its location to the church on the northeast side of town."

The Hunter looked taken aback, then shook his head. "We still need to clear the rest of the town, miss. It'll go faster if we split up into our respective groups. Or you can join the werewolves if you want, and head for the church. My men will do a perimeter sweep and work our way inwards."

Wolf crossed his arms finally giving off the impression of a werewolf leader. "Splitting up is dangerous. You can't treat this like you would a normal necromancer. Hell, even if it were just a normal vampire, it would be foolish."

Huck's expression flash disdain just for a moment, but Ruka saw it, and by their stiffening postures she could tell the werewolves did too.

"And just how many vampires have you fought against?" the Hunter asked, his tone overly polite.

"Oh I haven't, but this guy," Wolf clapped his hand on the back of Harris, "he's fought one before, and he says we'll need every last one of us in order to take it down."

There was silence as everyone processed. The last recorded battle against a vampire was nearly two hundred years ago, and in Europe. Did that mean there were more vampires alive than Ruka had originally thought, or was this man just very, very old?

"I see," Huck said, stroking his mustache to cover his discomfort. "Wish you woulda' told us that beforehand."

"Well, sometimes information gets lost in the pipelines," Wolf said, his smile stiff. "You understand how it is."

By the way Corporal Huck turned purple, and Ed and Archie glanced at each other uncomfortably, Ruka suspected they'd been less than forthcoming about sharing what they knew. She didn't particularly care about their issues, but wouldn't tolerate holding back information that could put her and her sisters in danger.

"And what sort of information might have already been 'lost in the pipeline'?" she asked lightly.

Wolf gave a shallow smile, still staring at Huck. "Well, it seems the Hunters already knew about this location. Seems this isn't the first team sent in, either."

"What's this?" Dusk broke in. She and Arabella had

returned from the car. "Are you trying to pull a fast one on us, Hunter?"

Ruka raised her brows at the captain. "Is this true?"

The Hunter scoffed as if they were being unreasonable, but wouldn't meet Wolf's eyes. "We had some data, yeah, so we sent a team to check it out, thinking it would be a false alarm."

"They didn't come back, did they?" Wolf asked, and when Ruka glanced over she saw his eyes showed flecks of amber.

"They didn't come back," Huck admitted, and hoisted his gun to chest level. "Which is why we asked for help from both your people. A threat like his affects all of us, after all."

"Very considerate, I'm sure," Arabella said in a scathing tone.

Huck shrugged like it wasn't a big deal. "We had no reason to tell you before since you weren't involved."

"Ridiculous!" Dusk said, throwing up her hands. She stomped back to the car, muttering under her breath about no-good, frog-spawned Hunters.

Wilson watched her leave with narrowed, snake-like eyes.

"Well," Wolf said, "we *are* working together now. Is there anything else you feel might the need to tell us?"

He spoke amiably, but Ruka could hear the steel in his voice. Huck, who seemed to take offence at the question, stared back at Wolf, his jaw set, and the two groups drew themselves up, neither wanting to back down.

The mission hadn't even started yet and they were already in conflict with one another. Should Ruka step in? She didn't want to take on the role of mediator and end up babysitting the two groups, but if their cooperation blew up now, it would be a disaster.

Tension mounted as the seconds ticked by.

"Wilson," Huck said, holding Wolf's eyes for one more breath before turning to his team member. "You and Ed get scouting. Everyone else finish your preparations. We leave in five minutes."

The Hunter turned on his heel, and the entire Hunter team retreated to their vans. Ed was the last to go, sneering with the puffed out pride of hot-blooded youth before turning and joining his cohorts. With a silent command, all werewolves but Wolf left as well.

"He's not telling us something," Wolf muttered. "Let's both keep an eye on those Hunters, I don't trust them.

"That's a given," Ruka said, and joined her sisters at the car.

THE OTHER WITCHES gathered around her trunk, pulling out their gear and helping each other kit up, weapons, artifacts and pouches checked and double-checked.

They took a side gravel road into town. Ed and Wilson left to scout, and it made Ruka uneasy having two Hunters out of sight, but decided the werewolves would know if they tried to double-cross the supernaturals. She didn't fully trust the wolves either, but was certain they'd work with the witches if trouble came.

"So, how many zombies can we expect?" Wolf asked while they walked.

He was on one side of her, and Captain Huck was on the other. Ruka wished they would both go away, but being a leader came with obligations. Unfortunately, one of those obligations was discussing strategy.

"I don't know exactly," she said. "None of my coven's texts could tell me much about vampires, and I've never even heard of a necromantic vampire. Perhaps Captain Huck knows more."

If she recalled correctly, one of her sister covens had several tomes on vampires, but it was a coven the Hunters raided several months back. It would undoubtedly take the Hunters some time to sort through and translate their spoils of war, but it was sloppy if they hadn't done so already, knowing what they were facing.

Ruka felt anger and disdain rise again at the thought of her sisters dying by their hand, and had to remind herself this wasn't the time or place to rectify past conflicts.

"Well," Huck said, "I know he's strong, uses magic, and is mean as fuck. We brought plenty of bullets, some silver. Put enough lead in him, and he'll go down."

"Vampires don't have a gender," Ruka informed him.

"It was a figure of speech, ma'am."

"So you're saying you know less about vampires than both the wolves and the witches," Wolf said.

The Hunter scowled. "If you have any nuggets of wisdom, feel free to share."

"Happy to," Wolf said. "Vampires require about one adult human's worth of blood a week at minimum to survive. The more energy or power it uses, the more blood it requires. It needs to be fresh, so you can bet it's keeping prisoners somewhere. Some will probably be kids, since that's what they prefer."

Ruka remembered the vision at the farm and swallowed.

"This is a necromantic vampire, so their needs will undoubtably be high," Ruka put in. "If I consider the magic needed to raise even a low level corpse, I estimate the vampire has killed half the village by now. Actually, it's probably killed the entire village since no one called the human government for help. Or have they?"

"Nah, you're right about that," Huck muttered. "The mayor apparently reached out, but law enforcement didn't think much of it and put them on the back-burner. Good thing, 'cause if word got out, shit would hit the fan. The village has, what, 2000 people? That's a lot. Still doesn't answer my question, though. How many stiffs will we be facing?"

"Well," Wolf drawled, "Harris told me they have the abilities of who they were as a human, only multiplied. The one he fought was a warlock. So some spells fizzled, and some packed a wallop. And by that I mean it took out an entire army platoon with one spell."

"'Kay then. So if a necromancer packed a wallop, what're we looking at?"

Ruka was already running calculations in her head. "Your average necromancer can raise six or seven undead. The most powerful one I've read about could handle twenty-two. If we use that number and multiply it by two or three times... Let's estimate seventy to be safe. It can probably raise half that again within a day if it pushes itself, so we'll bring it up to one hundred undead total."

"Sounds about right," Wolf said, brushing his brown hair away from his eyes.

"Fuck me, a hundred!?" The Hunter paled. "That's a lot more than we estimated."

"Considering you barely know anything about vampires, I'm surprised you were able to make any estimates at all," Ruka said.

"Ouch!" Wolf said, looking delighted. "Sweet and savage as ever." He slung an arm around Ruka's shoulder.

"Stop that," she muttered to him, her shoulders stiffening as Huck raised his eyebrows at them. She pushed Wolf's arm off. "By the Goddess, this isn't a date. We're going to battle."

"Yes ma'am," he said. He gave a saucy salute.

"Please call me Ruka, I'm not a ma'am. And if you'll excuse me, I need to talk to my sisters."

"Bossy little thing," she heard Huck say behind her.

"Oh, I know," Wolf replied, and the satisfaction in his voice made her cheeks burn.

Fear spread through the entire group after learning how many undead they'd be facing. And if they were right, and the vampire had already killed and feasted on half of the village's 2,000 residents, it would have plenty of bodies to replace the servants Ruka's team killed. Not a pleasant prospect, but at least magic would still be a limiting factor.

"That's a lot of undead," Nine said, thoughtfully playing with leather pockets on her hip holster. "Are you certain we do it?"

Dusk snorted. "Quit wetting your knickers, it's only a few servants. If Ruka's numbers are right, there's still sixteen of us. So, six or seven a piece? That's nothing. Back in my day—"

"Six or seven isn't bad, I agree," Wysteria agreed, "but that's assuming they're low-level undead. Higher servants can be tricky. Not only that, but we'll still have the vampire to face at the end of it all."

"We ration our magic, as always," Arabella said, sounding bored by the whole thing. "We don't have to fight the vampire today. If we kill its servants, we can pin it down in the village while we recover."

"The longer we draw it out, the more villagers will die," Nine pointed out. "And I don't particularly look forward to staying here while it's dark. The vampire is limited while the sun is out, but at night it will become stronger.

"True, but it's better a few humans die here than we all get killed and the vampire escapes and burrows into a city," Arabella said.

The way Arabella put it irritated Ruka, but it was an unfortunate and depressing truth. If they let the vampire escape, it surely would find a more populated area to hunt in, and in doing so, would make it much harder to kill than before. The witches might not even be able to find it before it showed up at their door.

"We won't let that happen," Ruka said. "Use your magic

wisely under the assumption that we must kill the vampire today. As unpleasant as they are, the Hunters and werewolves are well-equipped to do their part, so make use of them. Are we in agreement?"

"Yes, sister," Nine and Wysteria instantly confirmed.

Arabella agreed after a pause, followed by Dusk. Ruka had the distinct impression they were less than happy about having to take orders from her, payment or no.

The werewolves grouped up on Ruka's right suddenly stiffened and all looked in one direction. Ruka followed their line of sight but saw nothing to cause alarm.

Wolf called a halt, and they waited behind a bend in the road. Within seconds of stopping, Ruka heard running footsteps getting closer, and Wilson came into view through the trees, his skinny form sprinting for all he was worth.

"Incoming!" he hollered. "We have incoming!"

"Shit," Huck said, then yelled to the scout, "How many? And where's Ed?"

"They got Ed," came the reply.

Archie swore loudly, his hands moving to his twin pistols, and Doug's round face squished into an unhappy scowl. Ruka groaned. She would shed no tears for the loss of the youngest Hunter, but they were short on manpower as it was.

"And then there were fifteen," Nine murmured, calmer than even the older witches and wolves, who huddled together unconsciously.

When Wilson got close enough, Ruka could see a thick smear of brown blood across the front of his tactical vest. He took a second to catch his breath, and once calm enough, pulled a cigarette from his vest and light it with shaking hands.

"There's, uh—" he said, his sharp face sweaty and red, "—there's twelve -no wait, eleven. Eleven of the things. Ed took one out with his knife before they surrounded him. The bastards came out of nowhere."

"Twelve at once?" Ruka murmured to herself. "That's too many for a lookout."

"Was the vampire expecting us?"

The voice just behind her ear made Ruka jump, and she glowered at Wolf.

"Goddess, don't do that," she said. "As for your question, I don't know if it's expecting us. It may have simply posted servants at each road entrance into the village. We should be close to a gas station, according to the map."

"But you still think twelve is too many."

"Even if it has one hundred servants, twelve is far too many to leave at each road. There's..." She drew the map in her mind, counting. "Two gravel road entrances, plus the secondary highway that goes through East to West, and the main highway entrance to the South. It wouldn't make sense to leave many servants here. Did we make a mistake?"

Her stomach clenched at the thought.

"It might have left more here because of the gas station," Wolf said. "Or like I said, it could have been expecting us."

"Maybe," Ruka said, and straightened her shoulders. "Well, if it wasn't aware of us before, this first contact may have gotten its attention."

"It should be asleep now though, right?" Huck said.

"It should be," Ruka agreed.

"There seem to be too many unknowns here," Arabella said, pushing forward. "Why the hell doesn't anyone know more? I knew we'd be woefully unprepared, but this is borderline incompetent."

Anger flickered across Huck's face, and Archie spat on the ground.

Before the Hunters could reply, the female wolf, Denver, gave a sharp whistle to get their attention. Ruka saw figures flicker through the gaps in the trees, and then the horde came around the bend. They moved faster than she would have liked, almost at a slow trot.

"They're fresh ones!" Stan called, bringing his rifle up in a smooth motion that showed his years of military training.

The other Hunters followed suit a moment behind, dropping to one knee and pulling up their guns. The wolves shuddered as their bodies partially Shifted for combat, and around her, the witches sisters dipped their hands into pouches.

"Conserve your magic," Ruka reminded them, ignoring Arabella's mutters about stating the obvious, and slipped a hand into her own pouch. She drew out a small glass bead that twinkled with inner light, blessed with sunshine. It wasn't really sunshine, but a blend of fire, light and life magics, extremely effective on the undead.

Ruka held up the bead and waited until the first undead got within a reasonable distance. She gathered the tiniest bit of magic, drew it tight, and released it. The bead whistled through the air and buried itself in the lead undead's skull, destroying the brain and severing the necromantic connection.

"First kill to me," Ruka called in a clear, calm voice. "Hunters, you're next."

Huck gave her an annoyed look but signaled for his men to fire.

They were better than she'd thought. They weren't using silver bullets and several shots missed the head, but half of the undead were down within seconds.

"Witches now," Ruka called out. "Be careful with your shots."

The wolf Benny growled at her until Wolf cuffed his ear, and the kid looked abashed. "Let the witches use ranged magic, and once they get close enough, we'll finish them. Save your energy. It's going to be a long, bloody day."

Pleased by Wolf's sensible decision, Ruka waited while her

sisters each sent a bead whistling through the air. Three more undead fell, but a fourth only stumbled.

"Cats," Nine swore. "Mine aren't blessed, and it didn't hit the brain. Apologies."

"Our turn," Wolf said.

His four wolves strode forward, clawed hands held to their sides. They made quick work of the two undead remaining, and stood with gore-covered hands, looking pleased with themselves.

Benny sauntered back, pleased with their work. "That wasn't so bad."

Denver grimaced at her filthy clawed hands. "They're squishy, and they smell disgusting."

"You've smelled worse things," Benny joked.

"Okay, back to your places," Wolf told them, and they obediently trotted back.

"That was easier than I thought," Huck commented. "If it keeps on like this, we can finish up in a few hours."

The other Hunters seemed personally affronted by the undead, and after holstering Betty and Veronica, Archie made a show of kicking the downed bodies.

"That's for Eddie," he said, spitting on a corpse.

Ruka watched them with a derisive gaze. She appreciated their shooting skills, but now they were back to acting like immature frat boys.

"Don't get complacent," she said. "If the vampire knows we're here, it's probably raising more undead to replace these. We need to move."

Archie gave her the middle finger, and even Huck gave her a sour look, which was ridiculous. She wasn't responsible for the death of the Hunter.

Wolf came over. "Give them a minute," he said. "They just lost one of their men."

Ruka glared at him. "And they're going to lose a lot more if we stay here, venting our feelings. We need to kill that monster before it can build its forces. There will be time to mourn later."

"All right then," he said with a shrug. He turned to his men. "You heard the lady, let's move."

The wolves obeyed their leader, and the witches followed Ruka. Stan, Doug, and Wilson immediately followed Captain Huck, but Archie had to get in one last kick or two before trotting to catch up.

"Sorry about that," Huck said, coming alongside her. "The first loss is always the hardest, you know?"

He was trying to get her to lower her guard with his chummy display of one leader confiding in another. It wouldn't work.

"My condolences," Ruka said, feeling absolutely no empathy. "Now, which path do we take to the church? The shortest route is Buck Avenue, but it goes through housing. 12th Street is longer, but it's all paved road and will avoid most of the population."

"I recommend the longer route," Wolf said. "I don't want residents to come out and see what's going on."

Huck nodded. "I second that. Less population is always a good choice."

"It's decided then," Ruka said.

"Right," Wolf said. "Hunters should lead, with the witches behind them and werewolves making a loose circle to the sides and back."

Huck stroked his moustache in thought, then nodded. "Me and my men will be the assault force with three witches as backup," he said. "I suspect the vamp will send his zombies to flank us, or bring some sleepers in from the perimeter, so your guys can hang back and catch any of those."

Wolf shrugged, not bothered by Huck acting like it was his idea. "Fine by me."

"I'll be part of the assault team," Ruka said sweetly. Mindful of the instructions the Mother gave her, she wouldn't let go of the chance to display the power of the witches.

Huck gave a smile that was anything but happy. "Of course."

"On second thought," Wolf said, "let's include two witches on the assault force and one werewolf. You'll need a powerful melee fighter."

"Let me guess, you're volunteering yourself?" Ruka asked.

Wolf's grin was all the answer she needed.

7

———

The morning sun shone brightly overhead, but its cheerful light was in stark contrast to the eerily barren streets. Nothing moved.

Trees rustled in the slight breeze, but there were no other sounds; no birds chirping, no car engines running, no doors slamming or neighbors calling out to each other on the streets. The streets were empty save for splotches and sprays of dark brown she suspected was blood, and she couldn't shake the feeling that someone - or something - was watching them. It made her itchy to keep moving.

The group stopped and pressed their backs against the wall of the town's post office, staring at the church, which sat kitty corner across the street. At least two stories tall, it boasted a spire at the front and a modest bell tower at the back.

As in her vision, tall stained-glassed windows began fifteen feet up the solid white stone walls, showing scenes from the Christian bible in rainbow colors. The front doors looked to be heavy, solid wood, with no other visible entrances.

The church was practically a fortress, and Ruka could understand why the vampire chose it.

"Whadya think?" the Hunter leader asked, the bandana on his head already dark with sweat. He cradled his gun to his chest, shoulders tense. "I thought we'd see some resistance by now. We're only two blocks away."

"It smells," Wolf muttered. "The whole place smells like death."

Huck stroked his moustache and gave one of the ends a quick tug. "The sucker musta' moved fast to clear out the town. You think anyone got away, or are they all dead in a pile somewhere?"

Well that was a pleasant thought. Ruka shivered.

"We haven't seen any other undead, thought. Maybe it really did leave all its servants at the village entrances," Ruka murmured.

Wolf ran a hand through his hair in thought. "Let's not count on it. Harris, you take our wolves and the three witches to hide over there in case the vampire tries to escape out the back."

He pointed toward an open cemetery behind the church that took up a whole adjoining block, bordered by tall trees and thick shrubs. Harris gave a nod and beckoned for his group to follow. The wolves obediently followed, taking Dusk and Wysteria. After a look from Ruka, Arabella threw her nose into the air and stomped after them, her displeasure palpable.

Ruka sighed inwardly, then focused back on the church. "We deal with the vampire first, and then we can search for survivors."

All five Hunters, plus Nine, Wolf and herself waited while the other team travelled down the street and disappeared behind the furthermost shrubs. Wolf, who could communicate with his pack-mates through werewolf magic, nodded when they were in place.

Ruka pulled out her dagger and drew a glass bead from her pouch, forcing herself to show a calm exterior. Beside her, Nine readied a tiny pistol with silver bullets, effective on just about any magical creature.

"Let's go then," Huck said, and waved his men forward.

Huck took the lead, with Wilson and Doug right behind him, then Archie, who held his beloved revolvers in each hand, and the four of them shuffled up the cement walkway like heroes from an action movie. Wolf followed, with Ruka and Nine, and the ever professional Stan brought up the rear, his carefully schooled face betraying not a hint of emotion as he scanned the empty streets behind them.

Huck and Wilson took up places to each side of the thick oak double-doors and tested the handle, but found it locked. The Hunter Captain waved at Wolf, then the door, and the werewolf nodded in understanding.

Wolf slipped forward with a cat's grace and held up his hand to count down from three. At zero, he raised a foot and smashed it into the doors.

The bolt shattered and hit the sidewalk with a sharp ping, while the doors, forced inward by the violent kick, hit the inside walls with the sound of a cannon. All Hunters but Stan rushed inside, the ex-soldier calmly scanning the streets in case undead tried to sneak up behind them. Ruka, Nine and Wolf hurried forward as well, ready to kill everything inside.

There was no movement.

Wolf coughed and backed away, bringing his arm to his nose, and Ruka breathed from her mouth, the foul odor of decomposition coating her tongue and throat.

"Empty," he called. "No one's here."

Nine stuck her head in and immediately retreated outside. "I'll wait outside."

Ruka crept forward, not quite believing the vampire wasn't there. Several dozen bodies draped over wooden pews, with flies buzzing around, and at the far front, the pulpit was missing, just like in her vision. But unlike her vision, the coffin was conspicuously absent.

"You're right, it's gone," Ruka said after stepping back outside to catch her breath. This was disappointing, but not unexpected. She'd taken every precaution she could, but the vampire had known she traced it. The Mother was right, and her extra involvement had only created more problems.

"Well, that's a fucking bummer," Huck said. "What now?"

Wolf's eyes flashed gold, and soon his packmates came jogging to join them. Ruka was pleased to see Denver and Benny staying close to her witch sisters.

"This is why we should have swept the whole town," Huck complained, tapping his gun against his leg.

"Perhaps," Ruka said, unwilling to admit the Hunter may be right. "What next?"

"We should burn the bodies," Wolf said.

Huck scoffed. "Burn them? That's a waste of time. I thought you were in a hurry to kill the sucker."

Ruka tapped her hand against her hip bags, considering. "I don't know how far the vampire's magical reach is, but these dead bodies are time bombs. It would be unwise to leave them as is."

"Then *you* can do it. I'm taking my men to find the son of a bitch before he makes more dead bodies."

"It's moving!" Doug squeaked, stumbling back and snapping his weapon up in a panic. "One is moving!"

A lone corpse rose to its feet near the front of the church. It turned in a wobbly circle until it caught sight of them, then stretched out its arms and walked forward with a moan.

"Easy there, don't shoot it!" Wolf said. He nimbly made his way to the front and with one powerful swing ripped the undead's head off.

Everyone else stared at the other bodies throughout the

church, and a few tense minutes went by before it became clear no more were getting up.

"Does — does it know we're here?" Wysteria asked, smoothing hair back from her face nervously. She had retreated behind Benny, and the young man stood with his chest out bravely, unaware that Wysteria was famous in their Coven for her defensive spells.

"If it did," Huck said, "there'd be a lot more bodies gettin' up. Like I told you, it's sleeping."

Ruka observed the now headless body and sighed. "We should still burn them. The church is defendable if we run into trouble and need to retreat somewhere."

And she didn't trust the Hunters out of her sight. Who knew what trouble they could stir up on their own.

Huck seemed torn.

"Captain, we should go hunting while they clean up here," Wilson grumbled, squinting at the bodies through his greasy hair. "If we just kill the vamp, we don't need to worry about bodies."

"Hunters," Wolf said, a warning rumble in his voice, "I'll say this again. If we get split up, there's a greater chance we all get wiped out."

Huck scoffed. "Ya, well, maybe you don't have any balls, but I'm fully confident in the ability of my men."

"Says the man who already lost a team member," Arabella said loftily, and earned a dark glare from him.

"If we work together, we'll be done in fifteen, twenty minutes," Wolf said. He turned to Ruka. "Would it cost a lot of magic to burn them?"

"Not much," Ruka said. "If your men gather the bodies into piles outside, my sisters and I will burn them. You two can inspect a map and try to figure out where the vampire could have moved. It should be large enough to house its servants and human food source."

Huck grimaced, but after working his jaw a moment, finally gave in.

"Wilson," he called, and the Hunter trotted into the church to join them. "Get the boys to help drag these bodies out."

Wilson's eyes narrowed, but didn't argue with his boss's orders. Wolf didn't even need to give verbal commands, his wolves simply got up and started working. Ruka left Wolf and Huck alone to argue over a map, and within ten minutes, all the corpses stacked in piles on each side of the church.

"Nine, Dusk, help me," Ruka said. "Arabella and Wysteria can work on that pile."

They cast spells for burning, turning each pile into ash and bone fragments. It took more magic than she'd expected, and Ruka grimaced at the expenditure. There was no helping it, though. The bodies were just too fresh.

Ruka approached the other two leaders, who seemed to have come to an agreement. "Any luck?" she asked.

Wolf greeted her with a welcoming smile. "We think the high school is the best bet."

"The library is a second option, but the high school is bigger. According to Harris over there, suckers value square footage," Huck added.

"They're in opposite directions, though," Wolf said, "so we wanted to get your input before choosing."

By the look on Huck's face, it had been Wolf who insisted they get her opinion.

"Then I agree. The high school seems our best option," she said, hoping this wouldn't be another fruitless effort.

"Let's head out," Wolf said with a stretch.

Huck held up a hand. "Hold on there. You wolves may recover immediately, but my men need a chance to rest."

"A fair point," Ruka agreed, relieved he'd brought it up first. "I wouldn't mind a chance to recover some of the magic we used."

Wolf sighed. "Well then, if the ladies need some time, that's what we'll do."

Huck snorted. "Fifteen minutes to rest, everyone! Wilson, and Stan, you scout the path to the school."

Ruka looked at Wolf with alarm. She'd let the Hunters go off scouting the first time, and Wilson had brought back a small horde. Now that they were in town, if he made a mistake, he could bring back a significantly larger number. She nudged Wolf in the ribs.

"Uh, let's have Porkchop go instead of Stan," Wolf said. "Better ears, and better for close encounters."

Huck looked like he'd eaten a lemon. "Fine," he said. "Wilson, take the wolf with you. You see anything - anything at all - you get your ass back here."

He gave his subordinate a look to stress the point, and Wilson returned it with a two-finger salute. "Will do," the scout said.

Porkchop was unhappy, but left the church with Wilson. Relieved, Ruka sat down to meditate.

RUKA CROUCHED behind a row of parked cars with Huck and Wolf, observing two undead who stood guard at the front entrance of the high school.

"How many entrances are there?" Ruka whispered, hands hovering anxiously over the pouches at her waist.

Huck stroked his moustache. "Dunno."

Wolf peeked out again, then drew back. "We don't have enough people to cover them anyway. Behind the school is an open field, so if my wolves hide there, they'll be able to see anything trying to escape."

"Alright," Ruka said. "We'll keep it simple and use the same plan as the church."

Wolf left to relay orders and returned with Nine and the other four Hunters.

"Let us kill them," Ruka said, indicating Nine and herself. "Guns are loud, and if the vampire is here, we'd lose the element of surprise."

Huck and Wolf agreed, so Ruka and Nine crept as close as they could while staying out of sight. Catching the other witch's eye, Ruka handed over a bead of sunlight and readied one herself.

They both poked their heads up and released the beads, hearing them whistle through the air. Ruka allowed herself a pleased smile when both zombies collapsed. She waited a moment to make sure they wouldn't get up, then signaled Wolf and the Hunters.

As soon as she was inside, the unmistakable aroma of sickly rot floated through the air. Offices were just to the left, separated from a shabby seating area by a counter. A corridor lay ahead, stretching to the left beyond the offices, and to the right where it met up with a hallway lined with lockers painted a drab teal.

Aside from the glass walled entrance, the only other light was from a few fluorescents, likely left on for security or janitors. Ruka could make out the walls and doors if she squinted, but otherwise it was impossible to distinguish one shape from the next. A quick pinch of powder and muttered spell gave Ruka night vision, which helped her see, but it didn't help the dread she felt worrying about what awaited them beyond those hallways.

Wilson, Doug, and Archie drew closer to Huck, and even Stan and Nine showed signs of nervousness.

"This is a big place," Huck said. "Left or right?"

"Right," Wolf said immediately. "The smell is stronger to the right."

"Great," Doug muttered, licking his lips and flexing his chubby fingers on his gun.

"The werewolf and I go up front," Huck said. "Then Wilson, Archie, the witches, Doug and Stan to bring up the rear."

"Nine and I stay at the front as well," Ruka said firmly.

She still didn't trust the Hunters, not even a little, and though Wolf made her uncomfortable, she could at least depend on him. Huck looked like he wanted to argue, then shrugged, acting like he didn't care.

The trip down the hall was like something directly out of a horror movie. Blood sprayed the red brick walls and binders, backpacks and loose leaf papers covered the hard tile flooring, all caked in thick blood and entrails. On the right set of lockers, Ruka passed a single smeared handprint of blood, dark red to contrast the ugly green of the locker. Despite the mess from a hurried escape attempt, she didn't see a single body. The Hunter's booted footsteps echoed against the sinister, eerily empty hallway, and they gripped their guns like they were afraid of losing them.

Ruka held a pinch of wood ash and gunpowder, just in case they met a group of undead. Bullets were fine and well, but sometimes, explosives were the only solution.

Wolf stopped. "You hear that?" he asked.

Ruka squinted ahead at a glass trophy display case where hallways met in a T-intersection, listening hard. "No. What did you hear?"

He tilted his head. "It sounded like a voice calling out."

"Are you sure it was a living voice, and not one of those zombies?" Archie asked, the whites of his eyes and teeth standing out against his shadowy face.

Wolf tilted his head the other way, concentrating. "I don't..."

As his voice trailed off, everyone held their breaths. Ruka heard nothing, but Wolf slowly turned to stare at the left hallway junction. Yellow crept into his irises and he lifted one hand, twitching his fingers for the others to follow.

Stan ran a hand over his crewcut then motioned for Wilson to help cover the right hallway. The rest went left, and they came to a set of steel double doors. A small wire-enforced window was set into each door, and when Ruka leaned to get a look past Huck's wide shoulders, her pulse jumped.

It was a gymnasium, illuminated only by a row of small windows near the ceiling on the wall opposite the doors. Ruka could see a basketball hoop near them, and a scoreboard below the windows. But more importantly, she could make out a mound in the middle of the large room.

"Are those bodies?" Nine whispered.

Doug's breathing audibly picked up, and he crowded forward until he was practically pushing the two witches. Ruka felt like elbowing the mouth-breather, but Wolf stiffened.

"There it is again," he said. "There's definitely someone calling for help in there."

Her hands were clammy, and her throat tight, but Ruka forced herself to clear it. "We need to go in then," she whispered.

"You fuckin' crazy?" Archie drawled, and at the same time Wilson shook his head emphatically.

"That there is a BIG, mother fuckin' pile of bodies, and they could all be zombies," Huck said. With them all pressed together, Ruka could smell a hint of old spice mixed with sweat. "Stan, what do you think?"

"I think we need to go in now, sir," he said to Huck in a low, no-nonsense voice. "Ms. Nine can hold the door and keep holding it if we need a quick escape. There's no movement so far, so if there are any zombies, they haven't noticed we're here. The rest of us go in hard and fast, before they know we're here."

"Good man," Huck said, clapping Stan on the shoulder. "I knew I could count on you. We go in, then."

Ruka clenched the powder in her hand. "If there are many undead, I have a spell that can kill a large portion of them."

"I'll guard the hall too," Wilson volunteered quickly. "Don't want them sneaking up behind us."

"Good thinking," Huck said. He took in a deep, nervous breath. "Guess we should get in there."

Ruka grabbed a larger pinch of wood ash and gunpowder in case the body pile turned out to be a trap. Her left hand took a stone the size of a robin's egg, a glow stone artifact wrapped in gold wire, and cancelled her night vision spell.

"I'll give us light when you open the door, so be careful of your eyes," she whispered.

Huck gave her a sloppy salute and gripped the door handle. "Here we go. Three, two, one..."

He pulled open the door with ferocity, releasing a cloud of fetid air that made Ruka nearly gag, and the five of them stormed inside, leaving Wilson and Nine behind to guard. The moment she was in, Ruka threw the lighting artifact as high as she could, and the gymnasium burst into light.

What they saw was horrifying. It wasn't just a pile of bodies. They were arranged almost in a pyramid, with some even hung by a rope from the rafters high in the gym's ceiling, dangling over the pyramid's peak. It was beyond gruesome, and almost artistic.

"What is this?" Stan whispered, even his normally professional facade cracking.

Doug began to sniffle, and Ruka turned to see him trembling, and he pedaled backward to vomit against the gym wall. She was tempted to vomit herself, but her pride and anger forced her to hold it in.

"Geez Louise," Huck said, looking around with a stunned, disbelieving expression. "Geez Louise."

The pyramid held men, women and even children, laid on

top of each other with care. They almost looked like they were sleeping.

"Do we... do we need to burn these too?" Doug asked. He'd finished bringing up his breakfast and hovered uncomfortably close, his face green but still holding his rifle.

"No, not these ones," Ruka said. "

Archie glared at her. "What, you finally realize it's pointless?"

Despite her efforts to look calm on the outside, on the inside Ruka felt as shaken as the rest of them looked, and her hands itched to slap Archie's obnoxious face. "No. It would be better if we could," she told him, "but we can't spare the magic. We'll lock them inside. Wolf, do you hear the sound from earlier? These people are all dead, so I don't know where the voice could have come from? Perhaps we should check the bodies just in case."

"First, we should find something to brace the doors," Stan suggested. "Let's secure the area and then check the bodies."

"Excellent plan," Ruka said. "Wolf, could you ask one of your people to bring Arabella? She can use magic to brace the doors."

Wolf nodded and his eyes glazed yellow for a second. "On their way," he said. He stared at the pile. "Who's going to check the bodies?"

"No way in hell am I doing it," Archie said, his hands tapping his gun handles.

"Hey," Wilson called from the door. "How much longer? It stinks to high heaven, and we still have the rest of the school to check."

Nine flicked her eyes warily into the hallway beyond.

Personally, Ruka now doubted the vampire was in the high school at all. The macabre display didn't serve any purpose for the creature, which meant it was likely it had set this up just for them. Had it been bored, or did this elaborate presentation have some purpose she couldn't figure out?

One of the bodies twitched and Doug gave a high-pitched shriek, brought up his gun muzzle and began to spray the pile with bullets.

"Stop, Doug!" Huck hollered, immediately dashing for his subordinate, but Doug was too terrified to hear him. "Cease fire! I said to cease fire, dammit!"

Huck came up behind the Hunter and yanked him sharply backward. Doug fell right over and scrambled backward on his hands and feet before snatching his gun back up and aiming it at the pile again, this time without firing.

"Fuck," Huck said, his face flushed.

Wolf had already sped past them and was at the pile, moving limbs away. "Someone is alive in there! Come help me get him out!"

Huck moved to help, and Ruka saw his shoulders stiffen once he got close. "It's Everette," Huck said. "Boys, come help, it's Everette!"

Ruka peered at the pile, confused. "Who is Everette?" she asked.

"A Hunter from one of the missing teams," Stan said over his shoulder, his back straining as he heaved a dead woman out of the way.

They managed to pull the Hunter out to his waist, but had to stop when he screamed in pain. "The mo-monsters broke my leg," he sobbed. "They buried me under here. I don't wanna die. Please God, I don't wanna die."

Ruka swallowed, and Huck waved everyone back.

"Shit," Huck said. "We'll need to pull off all the bodies on top to get him out."

Archie moved to help again but then yelped and flinched back. Ruka gasped as one of the bodies in the pile came to life, tackling the missing Hunter and sinking its teeth into his neck.

"No!" Huck yelled, beating on the thing's head with the butt of his rifle.

He stopped bashing when Stan skidded in and tried to pry the undead's teeth opening using gloved hands, the muscles on his arms straining as he fought the thing's strong jaw.

"Get Everette out and put something against his neck!" Stan hollered.

Archie's hands fumbled as he ripped open a velcro pocket and pulled out a bandage. He didn't even bother unrolling it, just pushed the whole thing against the injured man's neck, blood pouring down his wrists as he tried to staunch the flow.

Huck finally pulled Everette free from the undead's teeth and Stan let go, taking a knife and ramming it into the undead's brain through its ear. Ruka bustled in, her fingers moving to free on of the health potions on her bandolier.

But it was too late. Blood burbled from Everett's mouth, and his eyes drooped and glazed. Sighing, Ruka pushed the healing potion back into place.

Huck spun away, ripping off his bandana and throwing it to the floor in frustration. "No, you — fuck! Shit! We had him! We had him, and the fucking asshair ripped his throat out."

Arabella arrived, along with Porkchop. The two of them eyed the pile of bodies with disgust and horror, their gazes flickering uneasily at the irate Hunters. Ruka quietly explained what had happened, as well as her plans to lock the remaining bodies inside.

"I'm surprised a survivor was left," Arabella said. "But I disagree about leaving the bodies alone. One already animated. If the vampire turns any of them into high servants, magical locks would be pointless."

"I understand that," Ruka said, feeling her patience eroding, "but it would cost us too much."

"We can always recover our magic," Arabella insisted stubbornly.

Ruka glanced around to see if anyone was witnessing their argument. Fortunately, Huck was going around talking to each of his men and Wolf was in quiet conversation with Porkchop.

"Not if we hope to find and kill the vampire before dark," Ruka replied to Arabella more snappish than she intended. "We still don't know where the vampire's lair is, and we haven't even come across more than the undead at the gas station, and the few here and at the church. I would prefer to burn the bodies as well, but that's a risk we'll just have to take."

Arabella's lips pinched, and she glanced at the bodies again. "Fine," she said. "But if this comes back to bite us, don't say I didn't warn you."

Her sister was truly getting on her nerves. Ruka understood that her sisters may have opinions that differed from hers, but to openly question her in front of the Hunters and werewolves was pushing it.

Wolf had finished talking to Porkchop and approached, rubbing a frustrated on the back of his neck. "So Now what?"

"We clear the rest of the school," Wilson called, still hovering by the door with Nine.

"No, the vampire isn't here," Ruka said.

"We don't know that for sure," Stan said, dropping his customary 'ma'am'. The soldier was still sitting by the pile of bodies, looking grim and tired.

"If it was here, we would have been swamped the minute your man Doug started shooting," she said.

Archie looked like his temper was flaring up again.

"Okay, let's all hold up. We need to take time to regroup," Wolf said. "Let's head back to the church for now. After seeing this, I think we should rest and figure out our next move."

Huck picked up his bandana and retied it around his head. "Fine," he said. "Lock the doors like we planned, and we head back to the church. That blood-sucking bastard is still out there, and we gotta figure out where soon."

"Before nightfall," Ruka agreed, "when it wakes up and becomes even more dangerous."

Arabella helped Ruka lock every door going in or out of the gymnasium, even the one that lead to adjoined bathrooms. Once done, the entire group met back at the front of the school, shaken and mentally exhausted. Now that Ruka thought about it, maybe that was the vampire's plan all along. The display in the gym had certainly worn away their nerves and morale.

The Hunters and wolves jumped at every minor sound and even Arabella was too jittery for sarcastic comments.

"The vampire isn't here," Ruka said once all groups were reunited. "We're going back to the church to rest and figure out other locations the vampire could be hiding."

"We don't have any clues?" Wysteria asked, gripping young Benny's arm with one hand, and a pinch of granite and comfrey powder with the other.

"We found a survivor," Wolf said, "but... We didn't make it in time."

Archie spat on the ground, his face dark.

"Why don't we just cast a search spell?" Arabella snapped. "Enough with this wandering all over town."

"That's not wise," Ruka said. "I cast one at the farm and it didn't end well."

Arabella rolled her eyes but didn't push. Thank the Goddess, Ruka didn't feel up to another argument.

"Hold up," Wilson called, and Ruka turned to see his attention on something down the road. "We have a zombie incoming."

"Just one?" Nine asked with raised eyebrows. She moved closer to Ruka. "Something feels wrong. Even if the vampire is keeping many of its servants in its lair, we should have seen more undead by now. Where are they all?"

That was a good question. One Ruka turned over in her mind while she watched Archie, Wilson and Huck surround the lone undead, taunting and kicking at it like bullies in a schoolyard. Wolf and the other werewolves looked on with disapproval, but made no effort to stop them.

"Enough," Ruka said. She stepped forward, took a glass bead from her waist and sent it through the undead servant's skull.

"The hell? We had it covered, witch," Archie said, giving her a look filled with disdain.

Ruka was thoroughly tired of dealing with Hunter's stupidity.

She looked coolly down her nose at Huck. "Control your men, Captain."

"Now look here, lady," Huck started, but Ruka had stopped listening.

She felt magic rising and spun to see Arabella in the center of a hastily drawn rune at front of the school entrance. The older witch hadn't put in any protective measures at all.

"No, wait Arabella! Stop!"

It was too late.

Ruka watched in horror as the rune lit up with magic. To interrupt now could be deadly.

"She's doing what we should have done in the first place," Dusk said. "Good line work too."

"It's a vampire," Ruka snapped, rushing over, "and Arabella didn't include any symbols to keep it from taking control of the spell."

She paced anxiously as the magic built, her arms wrapped around herself.

"It might be okay," Wolf said just behind her. "It's midday, the vampire is probably sleeping."

"What if it isn't?" Ruka asked, unable to take her eyes off Arabella.

The spell was approaching the climax, and with a rush of

power, completed. A wave of magic roll over Ruka and beyond, spreading through the town.

Everyone held their breath.

"So?" Huck asked, looking on with curiosity. "Did it work?"

Arabella was still in the center, slumped in the same seated position.

"I don't know," Ruka said, and drew in a breath when the witch sat up and opened her eyes.

"I found it," Arabella said, placing a hand against her chest with a triumphant expression. "An old building on the edge of town. It looked like an abandoned asylum."

"There we have it then," Dusk said. "Problem solved. We should have done this in the first place, I'm telling—"

Without warning, Arabella stiffened, and her back arched. Her mouth opened in a soundless scream and everyone watched in horror as her skin turned gray from the inside out, shriveling until it clung to her bones, paper-thin.

"No! Arabella!"

Ruka ran forward, holding her sister's body as it collapsed. She checked for a pulse, but felt none, and when she used her magic to detect for life force, discovered that no hint remained. Arabella was dead.

"Damn," Huck said, taking a step back. "That's not good."

"That's an understatement," Wolf said, and then he and every other werewolf dropped into a crouch, spinning in circles and growling loudly, their eyes bright yellow.

With a shiver, Ruka heard it too: banging and groans sounded from the houses surrounding them.

The first undead came out from a house a block down the street from the high school. And then another. And another. They poured out of the houses, one after another, stumbling over each other, tumbling into the streets.

"They're everywhere," she breathed, terrified tremors racking her body.

Within minutes, undead bodies filled the streets. Not just fifty or a hundred. Many hundreds. They crowded lawns, shop fronts, sidewalks and streets. As one, they all turned toward Ruka and her companions, shuffling toward them in hordes.

"Get into the high school!" Huck yelled, then swore in a long, creative sentence.

Ruka looked past her shoulder to see more undead banging bloody hands against the glass entrance walls.

With the bitter taste of fear and grief in her mouth, she released Arabella's body. "Back to the church! It's defensible!"

"The church is two blocks away!" Wilson called. "We won't make it."

"Oh yes, we will," Ruka said, gritting her teeth and rising to her feet. She reached back into the pouch of ash and gunpowder.

The time for caution was over.

8

———

Ruka rushed into the street, her heart in her throat as the never-ending stream of undead drew closer, their grey, bloated hands outstretched. "Dusk! Come create a barrier, around me, quickly! Nine and Wysteria, form one around our people!"

Nine and Wysteria jumped into action, drawing a large circle around the group of Hunters and werewolves with panicked motions. While Dusk hobbled over, Ruka used salt to draw a small circle around herself. She finished the outer circle and was working on one of the four inner ones when the old witch arrived.

Dusk immediately helped finish the inner circles and quickly sketched the symbols for protection. With the undead almost at the outer salt line, she held her hands up, muttered a quick incantation, and clapped her palms together. A barrier of rich blue shimmered into existence, just in time for the first undead to lunge at them. It hit the barrier and bounced back, almost knocking over more undead behind it.

"Ruka, what do we do?" Wysteria's called.

Her voice held a note of panic, and relief shot through Ruka when she saw their barrier was up. Unfortunately, nearly a dozen undead already gathered around them. Inside the circle, the werewolves growled and snapped at the animated bodies outside. Archie and Stan's guns wavering from head to head, overwhelmed by the targets surrounding them. It seemed they knew enough about witch barriers not to shoot, since nothing could enter or leave, but still kept their rifles up. They were safe for now, but the barrier wouldn't hold out indefinitely.

"I'm going to create an opening," Ruka said, almost yelling to make herself heard over the frenzied moans of the undead. "Then I'll burn a path to the church, but everyone will need to keep the undead off our sides and rear. If you have artifacts, now is the time to use them."

Ruka saw Wysteria give her a thumbs up. In one hand, Ruka took a loose fistful of ground dandelion seeds and a small calcite wand hanging from a leather strap on her hip. Since she was using an artifact, she didn't need to draw a rune, but gathered enough power to boost the magic of the wand.

"Ready!" Ruka called out.

Sending a quick prayer to the Goddess that they all make it to the church unharmed, Ruka placed the wand into the palm holding dandelion seeds and, aligning her intention with the magic and components, tapped the bottom of the wand onto the ground.

A rush of air rustled outward, whipping her hair and skirts. Outside the barrier, the effect was even greater, a great gust of air exploding outward. It streamed over the other barrier, leaving the occupants untouched, but the undead received the full effect of winds strong as a hurricane, and they blew backwards like bowling pins.

The dandelion seeds had atomized, used up in the spell, and Ruka shoved the wand into her pocket, quickly pulling out a fistful of ash and gunpowder and one of her health potions. She'd only tried this once before, but the experiment had been successful and with undead still arriving from side streets, she had very few other options.

"When we lower the shields, all of you run behind me and guard the sides and back! At my direction, Dusk. Ready... now!"

The shield dropped and Ruka poured the health potion over the gunpowder ash in her hand. "Roken, vender shon, urzen, fehlette ed tang, huundah!"

From ash and alchemy, burn to ash, flesh and bone, from preserved life, until all power is gone.

Flame burst to life in her palm, and Ruka divided half her concentration between the spell and half on the patter of footsteps that rushed up behind her. The Hunter's weapons erupted in short staccato bursts, and Ruka thought she could hear Doug sobbing.

Once she was certain they were in place, she send a flare of magic into the spell, and flames blew out from her palm like dragon's breath, turning all the undead fifteen feet in front of her to blackened ash.

She moved forward into the gap the impromptu flamethrower spell created; the flame dwindling to a flicker until the undead pressed within six feet. Her magic rose again, flames gusting forward to create a path, then dwindling again. This continued, over and over, and it took nearly all of Ruka's concentration to manage the spell and walk without stumbling over charred bodies.

She couldn't spare a thought for the people in her wake; she had to trust that they'd keep the undead off her back and themselves alive until they reached the church.

Ruka lost track of time, her entire existence narrowed down to keeping the magic steady until the undead came near enough, pushing magic into the spell and destroying the undead who blocked their way, then carefully placing her feet one step after another. She moved as quickly as she could, but it felt like an eternity until she heard a voice in her ear.

"Almost there," Wolf said from just behind her. "Another half block and we can make a rush for the church."

Hope rose when she realized the church was just in front of her. By then, sweat had drenched her blouse and forehead, her arms shaking with the effort to keep the spell steady. She was tempted to release the spell and let the Hunters and werewolves do the rest of the work, but was afraid they wouldn't be able to handle it on their own. So she persevered until they came to the sidewalk leading up to the church.

"Get ready to run," she yelled, her voice sounding weak to her own ears.

The moment she released the spell, her knees turned weak, and only a hand gripping her arm kept her up.

"Come on, Ruka," Nine gasped, firing her tiny pistol at an undead who came too near. "Can you carry her?"

Ruka turned to find out who Nine was talking to, but in the next instant found herself picked up by Wolf. "I've got her! Run into the church!"

The next few seconds were painfully uncomfortable as Wolf ran toward the church, easily carrying Ruka in his arms. The second they were inside, he set her down gently on a pew, and ran back outside to keep the undead at bay while the others scrambled inside.

"Get the doors!" Wolf yelled, and his packmates and several Hunters rushed to help.

The wood had splintered around the lock, but the hinges on both sides were solid metal. Ruka grabbed some sawdust from a bag on her waist and muttered a spell, throwing it into the air. The dust disappeared, and from the wood knots twisted and grew, welding the two doors together and bracing them.

Huck, who had slammed his shoulder against the doors as soon as they were closed, stepped back. "Is there a back entrance? Any other way for them to get in?"

"On it," Nine said, and pointed at Benny and Denver. "Come with me."

"I'll help as well," Wysteria said, rising on shaky legs and brushing off her skirts.

The werewolves looked at Wolf, and when he nodded, they leapt over pews to catch up. A moment later, Ruka felt the stir of magic as Nine and Wysteria reinforced a backdoor. And just in time. The first thud hit as the four returned.

"Will it hold?" Wilson asked, staring warily at the back door.

"It'll hold," Ruka said. "But that creates another problem. We're trapped inside."

The others sat on benches or the floor, nursing bleeding wounds or just staring off into space with pale faces.

"Wait," Huck said, looking around. "Where's Stan? Stan?" His voice became frantic. "Stan! Did anyone see where he went? Did we leave him out there?"

"He didn't make it, Captain," Wilson said, sounding weary. "The fucking stiffs got him a block out. I saw him go down."

Huck's face went white, then purple, and he rounded on Ruka. "You and your fucking witches. You just had to wake the thing, didn't you? Now we got two more people dead!"

"Oh Goddess, Arabella," Wysteria wailed, wiping the back of her hand across her eyes. Benny placed a hand on her shoulder and she burst into tears, throwing herself onto his chest.

"Don't be stupid," Ruka told him. "The vampire's been aware of us this whole time. It was playing with us."

"Bullshit."

"You really think that a being who could do this—" she waved at the oak doors, raising her voice above the clamor of meaty fists banging on it "—wouldn't know when six humans and ten supernaturals enter its domain?"

"It wasn't doing anything until—"

"Enough!"

The command came reinforced with magic, and even Ruka winced under the pressure. Wolf stood tall, his eyes bright gold.

"Enough arguing. We need to figure out how to get out of here, destroy as many undead as we can, and kill the vampire."

Huck threw his gun onto a pew like a bratty child and plunked himself down, looking up at Wolf expectantly. "Well? I'm all ears. You got a way out?"

Wolf looked to Ruka. "Any ideas?" he asked in a softer tone.

Ruka rubbed her forehead with her hand, realized muck covered it, and wiped it on her skirt. "I can use area spells to get rid of most of this lot, but I won't have much left. There's a lot of undead out there, but it only looked to be eight hundred, a thousand tops."

"Oh, is that all?" Huck said.

Ruka ignored the sarcasm. "The village population is 2,000. At this point it's not safe to make assumptions about how many more bodies there are, whether he's risen all of them, keeping some in reserve, or if they're alive somewhere. I just don't know."

Harris spoke up. "Didn't see none of them fast ones, neither. Necromancer of this strength, it'll be havin' a few o' those stored as well."

Nine, who had wandered over, spoke up. "He's right. All the ones we saw were slow - lower servants. The higher servants will be much stronger, and possibly intelligent."

The young witch had done her homework. Ruka gave an approving nod, which earned a tiny smile from Nine.

"So we just wait here until they find a way to break through, or we starve?" Huck asked.

"Of course not," Ruka snapped. "We send a message to the coven asking for help. It's about midday, so there's a chance they can make it here by tonight."

Huck scoffed. "I ain't putting my hope in your kind, I'll tell you right now."

Wilson came back looking grim. "I just took a quick look around. No phone installed, no cellar or other entrances other than the back door. There's a ladder up to the bell tower, though. We could get onto the roof, pick them off from there."

"It may come to that," Wolf said, and turned back to Ruka. "You said something about a message?"

"Yes. I know a magic that can send a message to any witch powerful enough to receive it. I can tell the Witch Mother what we're facing and ask for help."

Dusk hobbled over, the lines of her face etched deep. It seemed Arabella's death and their current situation took the spitfire out of the caustic old woman. "I can do that," she said. "It's a humdinger and will take a lot of magic. If I do it, you'll be free to rain down fire on those monsters. I'm not good with offensive spells, but I can send a message and give the rest of you a good strong barrier."

Ruka nodded solemnly, emotion thickening her throat. "Thank you, sister."

The old witch gripped her hand for a moment, their eyes connecting, and an unspoken message passed between them. No matter what, they were witches of the same coven and they would guard each other's backs. Then the moment was over, and Dusk shuffled away to an unused corner to draw a circle for a rune. The sight made Ruka incredibly proud to be part of a coven of such powerful women.

She turned to Wolf hesitantly. "Will you join me on the roof? I want to get a better look at the situation and figure out how to eliminate as many as possible."

"I thought we were waiting for help," Huck said, sounding petulant. It seemed now that things weren't working like he planned, he just wanted to argue for the sake of arguing.

"Would you want your Hunter associates to walk into this?" she asked.

He swallowed. "Fine," he grouched. "Go up and look, then."

"If possible, I want to take out as many as I can before they arrive," Ruka said.

Wilson stood. "Can we stack some benches to see out the windows?"

Huck paused. "Ya, sure, that's a good idea," he said. "Doug, Archie, give the man a hand."

Now that one of their own had come up with an idea, the Hunters sprang into action, working together to stack benches in a wobbly staircase under one of the windows.

Denver, who moved to help the Hunters, stopped when Wolf put a hand out.

"Help Dusk," he told her, indicating the old woman who was struggling to push a pew out of the circle she was drawing.

Denver immediately jumped in to help while Benny consoled Wysteria and Nine. Porkchop just watched the Hunters - all but Doug, who had taken out a photo and was staring at it mournfully - who managed to stack the benches impressively high.

The ladder was in the far back, beside steel door welded shut with smooth, perfect seams. Nine did outstanding work.

"After you," Wolf said.

Ruka grasped the bottom rungs. "Thank you."

She worked her way upward, placing her hands and feet carefully so she didn't slip and fall onto Wolf, who was getting a face full of her muck-covered skirt. She paused halfway up.

"Are you okay down there?" she asked with genuine concern.

"Just fine," he said, batting away fabric. "Don't worry about me, the view is great from here."

"Incorrigible," she muttered, but a smile tickled the corner of her lips. It disappeared as soon as she began climbing again, the moans rising in volume the further up she got.

At the top, Ruka pulled herself onto a tiny covered platform. She squeezed over as much as she could to make room for Wolf, who had to duck to avoid hitting his head on the bell.

Peering out of an arch, Ruka had an excellent view of the town, and more importantly, a clear view of the massive undead horde swarming around the church like flies. If the noise was horrible, the stench was nearly unbearable.

"Gah," Ruka said. "Disgusting,"

She tore off a strip off a clean section of her petticoat, rubbed in some lavender buds from a pouch, and offered it to Wolf. If the smell was bothering her that much, it must be even worse for someone with a sensitive nose.

He took it with surprise and quickly tied it around his face. "Thanks," he said.

"You're welcome," she said, and made another for herself. "Now, let's get a better idea of what we're dealing with."

One at a time, they eased out onto the steep roof. Ruka slung a leg onto either side of the peak and shuffled her bum along. Wolf, who had excellent balance, simply walked out, and Ruka was both amused and jealous.

"Look at them all," she said, pointing at the seething mass below. "I think my first estimation was about right. Looks to be nearly a thousand."

Wolf squinted. "Are all witches good at counting?"

"It's part of our training," she said absently. It was all fine and well to escape the church, but after that where would they go? They had no clues as to where the vampire could be other than the 'asylum' Arabella saw. Remembering that she'd brought a map, she now pulled it from an inner pocket in her blouse.

"What else do you keep in there?" Wolf asked and grimaced

when she gave him a flat stare. "Sorry. I tend to be a smart ass when I'm nervous."

"Hmmm. Arabella said she found the vampire at an abandoned asylum, but I didn't see one when I did research of the town. Not that we had much time."

Wolf sat behind her and peeked over her shoulder. "Here," he said, pointing to something. "What's that?"

Ruka squinted at the tiny print. "Historic Pioneer Village," she read. "I don't think that's what we're looking for."

She crumpled the map in frustration.

"Don't worry, we'll find it," Wolf said.

"But not in time to save Arabella."

Wolf squeezed her shoulder. "I'm sorry," he said. "For the loss of your sister."

To her horror, tears rose to Ruka's eyes, and she wiped them away as fast as she could. "Thank you."

"Were you two close?"

Had they been? Ruka had little room in her life for friends, not even with the sisters in her coven. There was always work to do, and witches were as much opponents as they were friends.

Still, they were of the same coven, and each worked toward similar goals. Despite the bickering, the competition over resources or rare books, Ruka knew that if it came down to it, she wouldn't hesitate to show loyalty to her fellow witches. And though she couldn't speak for them, she was certain they would do the same for her.

"We were sisters," she finally said.

Wolf nodded like he understood, which he might. Werewolves in a Pack fiercely depended on each other, even more tight-knit than a Coven.

"There's no one else here," he told her gently. "If you want to cry, you can. I won't tell anyone."

Ruka sniffed and wiped her face again. "I'm fine," she said.

"There will be time to cry later. Right now, we need to save our people and get out of here."

"That's one of the things I like about you," he murmured. "Your honest determination. In my lifetime, I've seen so many powerful people let their pride and greed get in the way of what needs to be done. I'm old, Ruka. And I'm tired. Tired of the games, tired of being alone. I volunteered to go to the farm without backup, which was foolish since a werewolf had already gone missing. It was a terrible risk, even for my kind, but I just didn't care. To be blunt... I had given up on life."

She swallowed, suddenly overwhelmed by this conversation that had suddenly become dark and intimate.

Wolf laughed softly and his expression cleared. "But then, I met *you*. You were so bright, Witchy. So alive, so proud and strong. I thought to myself, that if there was a woman like you in the world, maybe life wasn't so bad after all. It might be bold of me to say this, but... thank you. Thank you for saving me. Even if we never see past today, I want you to know that I greatly admire you."

Ruka suddenly realized that Wolf was uncomfortably close, and even worse, she was choking with the effort to hold back her tears. "Well, if we make it out of this alive, you can admire all you want."

He grinned that mischievous, wicked grin, and she suddenly realized what she just said.

"I — What I meant was—"

"I know what you meant," he said, leaning forward. "And rest assured, I will hold you to it."

He was really close now. Ruka wanted to pull away and run, but where could you run on a roof, especially when a werewolf was blocking off your only means of escape. And if she happened to admire his beautiful eyes, there was no harm.

Ruka cleared her throat and looked away.

They were on a church roof surrounded by a thousand

undead, and all she could think of was that his eyes were beautiful. Goddess, she was going to turn into Wysteria at this rate.

She heard a rumbling sound and blinked as Wolf's cheeks turned pink. "Sorry," he said, leaning back, his eyes crinkling over the cloth mask. "I'm hungry. Denver has the food, I'll grab a bite once we get down."

A smile crept across Ruka's face, but she eyed him with some concern. A hungry werewolf was a danger to everyone around him, especially one who might be mentally unsound if his earlier confession meant what she thought it did.

"Perhaps we should all take a break to eat and get some sleep," she agreed. "It seems impossible in this situation, but I don't know when we'll get another—"

A shot split the air, louder even than the constant thrum of undead, causing both Ruka and Wolf to start. They craned their necks in the direction the sound came from. At the edge of town, from where they originally entered, a figure stood on top of the three story brick hotel.

The figure fired another shot into the air, then waved.

SEVERAL OF THE undead had already peeled off and started for the hotel. Ruka wasn't sure if the person was trying to divert some of them or just get her and Wolf's attention, but he'd accomplished both.

"People," she breathed, feeling hopeful as she watched the figure disappear into a hole in the roof.

"We need to go to them," Wolf said, his eyes fixed on the building.

About half of the horde had abandoned the church for the hotel, but there were still plenty who ignored the shots and kept banging on the church walls, trying to get in.

"Are you crazy?" Ruka asked. "It'll be difficult enough just to save ourselves."

"They might know where the vampire is," Wolf said, already on his feet and waking back to the bell tower like he was on a tightrope. "Come on."

He was crazy.

No, scratch that. She was crazy.

She remembered the very undignified thoughts she'd been having just a few minute prior and blushed. Well, at least after this they'd part ways, and she'd never have to see him again.

Then again, that's what she thought last time.

Stop it, she told herself. Deal with one thing at a time. Survival first, annoying werewolves second. The thought calmed her, and Ruka felt back to her normal self by the time her feet stepped on to the church floor. Wolf was already calling over the others, all except for Dusk, who was sitting in the middle of a rune lit with magic.

The Hunters seemed to have given up on their tower of benches. Archie sat up from where he was lying, and Doug crept forward with his gun cradled to his chest.

"We heard shots," Huck said. "What was it? What did you see?"

"People," Wolf told them.

Ruka held up a hand at their excited looks. "Their shots drew off about half of the undead, but now we need to go help them."

"Not a good idea," Wilson said, and Doug emphatically nodded in agreement.

"Look," Ruka told them, "we have almost no clues about where the asylum is, or even what happened in this town. They might have the information we need. We don't have to kill every undead out there, but we should at least connect with whoever it is."

"That's a big risk for 'might'," Wysteria said, but she looked thoughtful.

Porkchop offered Ruka a canteen which she took after a brief hesitation. The water was stale but quenched her thirst, and after a few gulps she handed it back gratefully.

"That's why I'm asking for volunteers," she said. "Some of us will go to the hotel and talk to the survivors. If we have to, we can stay there until help arrives. The rest of you will stay here. In case we're killed, someone needs to be alive to tell others what happened."

Everyone fidgeted, hesitant. Ruka understood. Leaving the church was an incredibly risky move, but she felt anxious and impatient to do something. It seemed safe here, but instinct told her it was only a matter of time before the vampire sent stronger servants for them, to crack open the church like an oyster and pry their soft flesh from its shell.

Ruka lifted her chin, refusing to give in to the fear. Better to die fighting than become easy prey trapped in a cage.

Several moments passed, and still no one stepped forward. Not even the werewolves, which surprised her. She'd thought Wolf would have used his dominance to push his subordinates into joining, but he made no effort to force them.

The silence became more and more charged, and just when she thought it was going to be only her and Wolf, someone stepped forward.

"I'll come with you," Nine said, and although she looked pale, her voice was firm.

Ruka strode over and took the woman's hands. While it made Ruka proud to see her courage, it also hurt to think of the risk Nine was taking. The witch was young and had so many years ahead of her.

"Are you sure?" she asked in a low voice so the others wouldn't hear. Well, the werewolves could hear, but Ruka was no longer worried about them. "There's a good chance we won't make it."

Nine lifted her head. "I was prepared for that when I agreed to come in the first place," she said, looking Ruka right in the eye. "Before I became a witch, I saw firsthand what evil can do if left unchecked. I am not ashamed of the weak human I was, but now I have power. The helpless girl of yesterday has helped form the competent witch I am today, and I will honor her by fighting with that power."

Her words struck something real inside Ruka's heart, and there was nothing she could say that properly acknowledged that kind of spirit and resolve.

"Thank you," she said, almost overwhelmed by admiration. It was incredibly humbling that the youngest and weakest of them was showing such bravery. Ruka felt almost ashamed that she'd agree to go on this mission for the promise of power.

"I'll come too. I'm old, but I fear what the vampire will do to our Pack more than I fear death."

Ruka turned to see a werewolf - Harris, the old one who'd fought a vampire before - raise his hand. Wolf's mouth lifted, and the two exchanged affectionate smiles, making Ruka feel like an outsider. Harris's smile transformed his face just like it did for Wolf, softening his plain face and making him almost handsome.

Seeing the two of them side by side only increased her suspicion that the two were related, which Wolf confirmed when he said, "Thank you, uncle."

"So that's four," Nine said. "Any of your bunch care to join us?"

The young witch directed the question to Huck, who crossed his arms.

"Maybe you'll make it there in one piece. Maybe the people there will still be alive, maybe they'll know something about the vampire. Or maybe not. I'm not risking the lives of my men for maybes."

"And what if I told you that the person we saw on the roof was a Hunter?" Wolf said slyly, laying out his trump card. "Probably from the first team you sent."

Had it been a Hunter? Ruka couldn't tell, but Wolf had better eyes than her.

Huck's entire body stiffened. "Oh?" he asked, trying to sound doubtful, but failing. "How could you tell it was a Hunter? And why should I believe you?"

Wolf's smile didn't show teeth, but was still predatory. "I could tell it was a Hunter because I could see him. Same tactical party outfit as the rest of you. And whether I'm lying.... There's only one way to find out."

The Hunter narrowed his eyes at Wolf for a moment, as if trying to read him, then waved his subordinates over. They spent some seconds in hushed argument until Huck broke it up and picked up his weapon.

"Wilson and I will come to the hotel. Archie, you're in command while we're gone. If rescue comes and we're not in breathing shape, you tell our people what they need to know."

It seemed to Ruka that an unspoken message passed between the two, and then Archie nodded.

Wilson, surprisingly, seemed completely fine with the decision, slinging a bag crosswise over his chest and grabbing his rifle. "When do we leave?"

Ruka raised her brows at Wolf, who said, "As soon as we have a plan on how not to die between here and there."

Wilson worked his tongue across his front teeth thoughtfully. "I might have an idea about that. Let's go back up top so you can see for yourselves."

Ruka, Nine, Harris, Wolf and Huck followed him up the ladder to the roof, and one by one, scooted forward along the steep peak, Huck muttered something about his balls under his breath. Repulsed, Ruka did her best to ignore him.

"Looks like they drew about half those rotten bastards off of us," the grizzled Hunter said, already sweating again.

It was early afternoon by then, and though it was still early summer, the sun was ferocious. Ruka was grateful her skirts, which cushioned her from the tiles' sharp edges and burning heat. She wished she could cast a breeze to cool herself, but still needed to conserve every bit of magic she could. Very little of this entire venture had gone to plan, and depending on how much resistance they faced going to the hotel, she was worried she'd run out of magic at a key moment.

"So the question is then," Huck muttered, "how do we get there without being chomped? If none of zombie bastards see us, we can make it there no problem. I think I saw an emergency ladder in the alley when we passed the hotel. We can get up to the third floor with that."

"A good idea, especially since the survivors have likely blocked access to the lower floors from inside," Ruka said.

"So we have an entry point," Wolf said. "How will we distract the undead surrounding us?"

"That part's easy," Huck said, and nodded at Wilson.

The skinny Hunter took a knife from his vest, pull up his sleeve and made a shallow slice on his tanned arm. He waited until blood welled up, then flicked it through the air. The blood flew in an arc that cleared the edge of the roof, and Ruka saw bodies clump together in the area as it landed. Wilson put a large bandaid on the cut, pressing carefully to seal the sticky edges.

"They like blood," she said, intrigued. "That's unexpected."

"Why?" Wolf asked.

"Undead rarely exhibit that kind of preference. Once they're aware of prey, they track them through life force, not physical senses - which makes sense considering many of their sensory organs had rotted - so being attracted to blood is unusual. Perhaps it's a trait inherited from their master."

"Well, it works pretty good," Wolf said. "How did you figure this out?" This he directed toward the Hunters.

"That's what got Ed," Wilson blurted. "He cut himself on something, and next thing you know, the stiffs surrounded him."

Once again, Ruka felt like something was off. But Wolf, who could detect a lie just by hearing it, didn't object, so she let it go.

"So, we get someone up on the roof and have them distract this horde long enough for us to sneak out the back door," Ruka said, and Huck made a sound of agreement.

"How will we draw the ones at the hotel away from the fire escape?" she asked.

"I'll do that," Wolf said. "I can act as bait and lead them away, then circle back and hop up the ladder to join you."

Ruka frowned, uneasy at the thought of Wolf putting himself in danger, but she couldn't think of a better idea.

"I can give you a warding spell," she said. "It's not infallible, but it could help you out of a pinch."

"Save your magic," Wolf said. "I won't need it."

She levelled him with a stern expression. "I insist."

Wolf held her eyes for long enough she wondered if she'd made a mistake and he'd take offence. Instead, he shifted his eyes down, a smile playing at the corners of his mouth. "If you insist then."

Harris glanced back and forth between the two with an unreadable expression, but fortunately, Nine and the two Hunters hadn't noticed the interchange. Ruka already felt awkward about how she felt about Wolf's obvious interest in her.

"Let's go back down," Ruka said. "We'll tell the others and get a volunteer for the roof."

Once their feet were back on solid ground and they

explained their plan, two of the werewolves agreed to serve as a distraction. Wysteria healed the cut in Wilson's hand, her nose turned up the whole time, and the rest of them made sure there were no nicks or open wounds that would get unwanted attention.

Wolf took a moment to down the beef jerky and candy bars Denver handed him. Ruka, who knew that a hungry werewolf was a dangerous werewolf, whispered that he should eat more, but he just gave her one of his silly grins.

"We only have so much, and they need food as much as I do," he told her. "And when was the last time you ate?"

Ruka recalled the four magic-infused granola bars in the pouch at her back. She took one out and munched on it under Wolf's approving eye, deciding to save the rest in case the werewolves started getting too cagey.

The party of six gathered by the back door and Nine removed the reinforcement while Wolf held his shoulder against it. Wysteria stood by to seal the door again after they'd left, and Archie waited at the top of the ladder, ready to inform them when the werewolves on the roof were in place.

"Starting now," Archie called down.

Ruka stood with magic tingling at her fingertips, her heart pounding and praying to the Goddess they weren't making a huge mistake.

The minutes crawled by, and just when she wondered if this plan was going to work, the call came down.

"Hey! Hey! Hey! They're all gathered up now," Archie hollered. "The outside should be clear."

Wolf eased away from the door and quietly unlatched the lock. The door opened without even a squeak, and although a stench of rot poured in, Ruka couldn't see a single undead.

"Let's go," Wolf whispered, and squeezed himself out.

9

"Disgusting," Nine muttered, her face wrinkling at the stench.

The whole lawn outside the church was slick and dark with body fluids, with unidentifiable clumps here and there that Ruka had to gingerly step around.

"We'll be clear of it soon," Huck whispered. "Don't slip."

Excellent advice, just in time for Ruka's foot to come down on something slippery, her leg nearly coming out from under her. Only quick intervention from Wilson saved her from landing in the muck.

"Thank you," she said.

He tipped an imaginary hat. "Ma'am."

They made it to the tree line safely and Wolf crouched down. His eyes flared yellow as he focused, and within seconds Ruka saw the undead spread out from where they gathered against one side. The werewolves on the roof finished their job.

"Let's go," he said.

Away from the clamor at the church, the streets were eerily quiet. Paranoia filled Ruka, like the window of every building was staring at her, with nefarious monsters tucked inside their shadows, ready to jump out and eat them.

Nothing did, however, and they made it to the hotel without running into a single undead, which instead of alleviating her nerves, only agitated them. A hiding spot behind a dumpster in an alley across the street gave them an excellent view not only the fire escape, but the hoard that surrounded the building.

"There are a lot of those buggers," Huck whispered.

Nine rolled her eyes at him stating the obvious.

Wolf breathed out through his mouth slowly. "Well, no time like the present," he said. "I'll go around to the opposite side to distract them. Harris can let you know when it's safe to go."

Ruka sent a quick plea to the Goddess to watch over them, and prepared to cast a warding spell.

"Hold up there," Harris said. "I think it might be better for me to go."

Wolf paused. "I've already decided to do this."

"I been thinkin' it's better for you to stay here," Harris said.

The two went quiet, but something unspoken passed between them, a silent conversation through their Pack magic that the others couldn't join.

Wolf ran a hand through his shaggy brown hair, then glanced at Ruka and swallowed. "Yes," he said, his voice thick with an emotion Ruka couldn't interpret.

"You boys made up your minds yet?" Huck asked. The Hunter rubbed his forehead against his arm to wipe off the sweat running down his temples.

"Daylight's wasting, and I don't wanna be here when the sucker wakes up from his coffin nap."

"We've made up our minds," Wolf said, looking grim.

Harris tried to stand, but Ruka made him wait.

"I can at least give you this," she said, and cast a magical shield on him. "It wouldn't hold against many, but can throw off a couple at least."

"Don't try to fight them," Wolf ordered, his brown eyes anxious. "Just run. Make sure you meet us back here in one piece, understood?"

"Yes sir," Harris replied, "that I'll do."

The wait after Harris left was excruciating. Ruka felt exposed and eager to get moving. The sooner they got into the building, the sooner they might have answers. At this point, any clue would be more than they had now. She poked her head out from behind the dumpster for the umpteenth time, wondering what was taking Harris so long.

After what felt like an eternity, the horde suddenly paused from beating their fists against the side of the building. A few focused their attention on something just out of Ruka's sight, and then they shuffled around the sides of the building, first a few, then more and more until a stream of undead poured around the corner and out of sight. Only a couple stragglers remained, too damaged to move as quickly as the others.

"That looks like enough," Huck said, but Wolf held him back.

"Wait. We need to give it enough time for Harris to take them far away. If we catch the attention of even a small group, they'll be in the way when he returns."

The Hunter's moustache twitched. "Fine," he growled. "We'll give him two minutes. Then we go, whether they're all gone or not."

The look in Wolf's eye turned dangerous, and Ruka watched with nervous anticipation as the last undead disappeared around the corner. Relieved, she stood and shook one leg then the other, trying to work out stiffness from her awkward crouch. Pins and needles set in but she ignored them, eager to get to the fire escape.

"Follow behind me, and keep close," Wolf told them, heading across the street in a smooth stride.

Ruka trotted to keep up, her skirts whisking around her

legs, with Nine at her side. The two Hunters came last, weapons swaying left and right as they scanned for the slightest movement.

The alley was as smelly and disgusting as the churchyard had been. Wolf asked Wilson to grab his foot to lift him up, but the Hunter took one look at the pulp caked to Wolf's shoes and pulled up an old milk crate instead.

The werewolf stepped onto it and pushed off in a giant leap, flicking his foot at the last second to send gore speckling onto Wilson's face.

The Hunter stepped backward hastily, wiping his cheeks. "Asshole."

Wolf, who caught the bottom of the fire escape ladder, ignored him. "I'll lower it as quietly as I can. Ready?"

"Here's hoping the building owners did regular maintenance," Nine said, looking upward.

The ladder gave an alarming squeak when Wolf pushed on it, and Ruka's heart surged to her throat. After the rough start, however, the ladder rolled smoothly against casters until it fully extended to the ground, the bottom landing in viscera.

"Up you go," Huck said to Nine.

The witch started climbing, and at the top Wolf grabbed her hand and effortlessly pulled her the rest of the way.

"Send your man next," Ruka told Huck.

"You don't need to tell me twice," Wilson said, and scurried up the ladder before anyone could protest.

"I'll go last," she said.

"Nope, you're next," Wolf said, and got on his knees looking down with his hand out. "I insist."

They didn't have time to argue, so Ruka climbed the ladder, and when she was in reach of Wolf's grip, found herself lifted into the air. He caught her by the waist and set her down carefully before turning to Huck.

"Don't need your help," Huck said, waving off Wolf's

outstretched hand, but added, "If you see any of those zombies behind me though, pull my ass up."

The others started up the stairs, but Wolf sat to wait for Harris, and Ruka stayed with him.

"Is he coming?" she asked, a thread of anxiety winding its way up her spine as the minutes ticked by.

Wolf nodded, his eyes yellow and unfocused. "I told him to come as soon as Wilson made it up. He's on his way now, but…"

"But what?"

"He feels afraid," Wolf said, and his eyes kept flashing yellow. "He's okay for now though. He's far enough — come on you idiot, come on."

Ruka put a hand on his arm, his muscles tense and hard as a rock.

Without warning, he got up and started pacing on the tiny platform. "He took a wrong turn," he said, and ran a hand through his hair. "They're going to surround him."

"He can still get free," Ruka said, the sight of Wolf's anxiety more terrifying than anything she'd experienced so far. "He can still make it."

She dove into a pouch and pulled out a handful of dried roots, drawing up magic to deal with the undead that would follow the werewolf.

"Come on, Harris, run," Wolf said, his eyes unfocused. "Come on."

He stopped short, all the blood draining from his face. Then he grabbed his head in his hands, nearly tearing hair out. "They got him," he said, his voice thick and in pain. "They got him. He's—"

Ruka let the magic fade from her hand, her heart aching. She pulled Wolf close to her with one arm and he buried his face into the crook of her neck, his breath coming in heavy gasps.

A voice called out, "Is he coming or what?"

Ruka looked up to see Huck peering down through several grated platforms at them.

"No," she called back, a pit in her stomach. "He's not coming."

She pet Wolf's head, ignoring the dried blood crusted on it. "Why didn't you break off your Pack connection?" she asked in a quiet voice, knowing he'd experienced everything Harris had at the moment of his death.

"I couldn't," Wolf said thickly. "I couldn't do that to him, or he would have died alone."

Oh Goddess. Ruka's her eyes prickled with tears. She swallowed them back.

"Let's go," she said. "There are people we still need saved."

Almost like he didn't want to, Wolf pulled back. His eyes were full of agony, but he hadn't allowed himself to cry, and Ruka watched him struggle to gather his composure.

"Okay," he said with a shuddering breath. "I'm okay now."

He pulled up the ladder, and then they climbed the stairwell as quietly as they could. Already the undead returned and a few gathered underneath them, their arms reaching up to grab hold of the living meals just out of reach.

When they made it to the roof Nine was there, scanning the horizon and glancing up at the sun with an anxious expression.

"I'm glad you're here," the young witch murmured. "What happened to Harris?"

Wolf's jaw tightened, and Nine nodded in understanding. "I'm sorry," she said. "He seemed like a good wolf. A good person."

Again, Ruka was struck by Nine's maturity and wisdom, and Ruka squeeze her hand in gratitude.

Several people surrounded Huck and Wilson, hanging on every word Huck was saying. As for Huck, he was smiling ear to ear, and it was no surprise why. Two of the survivors wore

Hunter gear, and Ruka watched a man with greasy hair and shadows under his eyes slap Wilson on the back.

"You three," Huck called, jarring her from her thoughts. "Come on over here, I want you to meet some of my guys."

Ruka greeted them, but Wolf hung back with Nine.

"Anderson, this is Ruka, the witch I was telling you about."

"A pleasure to meet you, ma'am," the Hunter said with a smile that didn't reach his eyes. Like the other Hunters she met for the first time, he eyed her with hostility.

"The feeling is mutual," she told him. "I'm hoping you can give us some information, both about the vampire and what happened here."

Anderson dropped his smile. "Of course. Let's go in, though. We're running out of supplies, but we still have some bottled water."

He led them to a hatch in the roof with stairs going down. "Man, are we glad to see you here. Much longer and we'd be out of both food and water. Most of it's on the lower floor where the zombies have been hiding. We've had to ration what we had the last couple days."

Ruka frowned. "Ration? How long have you been here?"

From the corner of her eye, she saw Huck's expression become wary.

Anderson sighed. "Since Wednesday, ma'am. We've been trapped in this damn hotel for three days."

Her inner alarm sounded. The Hunters had only asked her to investigate the farm two days ago. If they were trapped here three days, then the Hunters had known about the vampire a lot longer than they'd let on.

THE INSIDE of the hotel stank nearly as much as outside, but in a different way. Ruka ignored it as best she could.

A small group of humans stood in a clump watching, one of them a young man with bleached hair styled into a high swoop that fell over one eye. He brightened in appreciation when he saw her and latched himself to her side. "Uh, sorry about the mess," he said. "And the smell. There's only four rooms on this floor and none of the toilets work anymore, so they're pretty grody. I mean, no duh, right? Plus, the A/C is out. That sucks, you know?" He laughed, looking extremely self-conscious.

"So, um, are you guys part of a special SWAT force or something?" The kid eyed Ruka's dress, leather holsters and bandolier, his eyes lingering on her chest.

"No," she said, too tired and heartsick to react to this human.

"Right, right, I didn't think so." He laughed again and smoothed invisible strands of hair behind his ears. "So like, what are you? Cops? Or like, some badass ninja chick or something?"

"What's your name?" Ruka asked.

"Right, I didn't tell you my name, duh!" he said, smacking himself on the forehead. "I'm Michael. And you are?"

"Michael, my name is Ruka and I'm a witch. I'm twice your age, and am upset that thousands of people, one of my friends included, are dead. That man over there," she pointed toward the stairs and Wolf, who had just came down with Nine, "is a werewolf. He just saw one of his friends die, so I kindly ask that you leave him alone so he doesn't rip out your throat."

Michael's expression hopped from flirtatious, to confused, to wary. By the time Ruka finished talking, he was pale. After stammering an apology, he excused himself and wandered away to join the other humans.

"Captain Huck," she said, and the man looked up from a deep discussion with his fellow Hunters. "I need a word."

"Ya, in a minute," Huck replied, and turned his back to her.

"Now," she said in a way that conveyed ignoring her wasn't an option.

Huck exchanged a look with his buddies, then stepped away to join her.

"What is this about a Hunter team being sent here four days ago? First, you didn't tell us about a team at all. Then you tell us that one came here, but only recently. Now I find you had an entire four days' lead time, even before you asked us to investigate the farm. Just what game are you playing, exactly?"

She didn't realize her voice had risen until the conversation died down and everyone looked over. Wolf came up beside her.

"Jesus," Huck said, his jaw clenching. His eyes shifted back to the other Hunters who had picked up their guns and stepped forward threateningly. "Easy there, witch. I don't make the orders, I just follow them. I told you as much as I was allowed."

"Don't waste your magic on him," Wolf said into her ear, and Ruka realized her fingertips were tingling with power.

She flicked her fingers and let the magic died back down.

Huck backed away. "Give yourself a minute to calm down and then let's talk."

"You pompous—" Red filled Ruka's vison, and she raised her hand to slap him, but Wolf caught it.

Huck shook his head and returned to his group, who openly sneered at her with their hands on their weapons, the bastards.

Wolf guided her from the room.

"What was that about?" he asked. "It's not like you to lose your cool like that."

Ruka, who just began to calm down, found herself fuming again.

"Typical Hunter bullshit," she said. "The team that they 'sent just before us' has been here for four days, Wolf. Four!"

"Okay," he said. "We already knew they were lying to us, but it doesn't change the fact that we have people to save and a vampire to hunt down."

"You don't understand," Ruka told him. "They sent a team here before they requested me to investigate the farm. It means they already had an idea of what they were facing before I even got there. If they'd have been forthcoming about what they knew from the start, Arabella wouldn't have died. And maybe Harris wouldn't have either."

Wolf's face darkened, and he rubbed his eyes. "We can't act on just that. I mean, they didn't know it was a vampire, did they? As far as they knew, it was just some rogue necromancer, a little stronger and craftier than most."

Ruka scoffed and paced in the hallway. "The more I think about it, the stranger it seems. If their team disappeared here four days ago, why didn't they send me here first? Why the farm?"

"Because the farm was probably safer?"

"How would they know it was safer?" Ruka pointed out. "They lost one team at the farm a week ago, and the second team they lost here. Wouldn't you send people to the most recent attack first? There's a better chance of finding survivors and fresh clues."

"I... you have a point," Wolf said. "It's in their best interest to take this thing out as soon as possible, since the vampire is as much a threat to them as it is to us. Maybe more. They lost two active teams, which is no small thing for them, and the entire goal of the Hunters is to protect humans from supernaturals. It doesn't make sense that they'd sabotage themselves, does it?"

"You're right," Ruka said, a realization suddenly making her depressed. "The problem is that there's politics involved."

"What?"

She massaged her forehead, trying to stop the pressure from building into a full-fledged headache. "The Witch Mother has been pushing the Hunters for a peace treaty. My involvement was supposed to gain us several years of a ceasefire, provided the witches offer adequate assistance of course."

"Ya, that's our deal too."

"Let me guess, the Hunters approached you with these terms, not the other way around?"

Wolf blinked. "Yup."

"Why? You're enemies. The witches became involved because Hunters asked us to analyze the necromancer's magic, but why approach werewolves for help?" She began to pace in the narrow hallway. "I'm about to make some very dangerous conjectures. What if the promise of a ceasefire was to lure us to join this mission? What if we're not here to help, but act as bait? Vampires prefer supernaturals to humans, our blood is much more potent."

Wolf's eyes lightened in color and he rubbed the back of his neck. "You're saying that the Hunters are using supernaturals to help them with a foe they can't handle themselves, but don't intend to honor their side of the deal."

"If no witches or werewolves make it out alive," she said, "who's to say we played any part in the vampire's defeat?" She met his eyes. "I don't think the Hunters intended to let us survive no matter what."

Now Wolf's eyes were not only yellow, but fangs poked out from between snarling lips. "Those sons of bitches! They kept trying to split off on their own, probably to leave us to wake the horde while they tracked down the vampire," he hissed. "I'll kill them! I'll—"

"Wait," Ruka said, rushing to put herself between him and the room where the Hunters were.

"Right now, it's all supposition. Not only that, but we need the Hunters if we're going to survive this. We know - or at least think we know - what their plan is. Forewarned is forearmed."

"That doesn't help Harris," Wolf growled. "Or Arabella."

"I know," Ruka told him, feeling a heavy weight on her

shoulders. "But you still have packmates here. I still have my sisters to look out for. We're already down several people, Wolf. We're facing a thousand undead, possibly more, plus we have to fight the vampire itself. At this point, we need all the help we can get, and I don't have any proof they're trying to backstab us."

"Since when does a supernatural need an excuse to kill a Hunter?" Wolf asked. His eyes were still yellow, but he seemed calmer now. "They've killed enough of our kind, I won't cry over their deaths."

"I agree," she said. "But we'll make use of them first, in the same way I suspect they're trying to make use of us."

"You want them to become *our* distraction."

"I do. Their plan wouldn't have worked, anyway. The vampire knew we were here from the start, no matter what that idiot Huck thinks. If they'd have gone off on their own, they would have died. It's ironic that by insisting they stay with us, we ruined their plans but likely save their lives."

Wolf snarled again, but it was without heat and Ruka no longer feared he'd rush back and slaughter everyone.

She rubbed her eyes. "Okay. So then, all we need to do now is think of how to find the vampire."

"You still want to track it down?" Wolf asked.

"I do. My sisters are coming. If they come tonight, they'll be forced to deal with the vampire during nighttime. More likely, though, is that they'll wait until the morning, and by then we might all be dead. I want to kill as many undead as we can, and figure out where it is so that even if we don't make it, my sisters can succeed. Can I count on you?"

Wolf's eyebrows drew together in mock offence, then one corner of his mouth curled up. "Witch lady, I'm yours."

The way he looked at her when he said that took her breath away, and once again Ruka felt uncomfortably *seen*, like he was looking straight into her soul.

Someone started yelling, which broke up the moment, and both Ruka and Wolf hurried back to the room.

"What is it now?" she asked.

Michael tumbled down the stairs from the roof. "They're going away," he said, pointing upward. "The zombies, they're all leaving the hotel."

"What?" Nine asked, standing up from the floor where she'd been meditating.

Off in their own corner, the Hunters looked confused and alarmed.

"Where are they going?" Huck asked, heading to the stairs.

"They — they're headed back to the church," Michael said.

Ruka's heart sunk. She had a very, very bad feeling.

10

R uka ran after Wolf, joining the others at the very
edge of the roof. Their eyes were glued to something
in the distance, and when Ruka squeezed up beside
them, she gasped.

The entire horde was swarming around the church, and
unlike the sluggish movements before, they clamored in a
frenzy.

"Did someone try leaving?" Huck asked, baffled. "The
dumbasses. I told them to stay put. If they—"

"That's not it," Ruka said, and raised a finger to point.
"Those are higher servants. The vampire is making a move."

Four dark figures were actually climbing the side of the
church like spiders, inching their way up the walls toward the
stained glass windows. The sight caused Ruka's heart to pound
so hard she could feel it behind her eyes.

"No," she whispered, dread making her dizzy. "We have to
warn them!"

"I already did," Wolf said, his voice strained.

Even as far as they were, even over the undead's constant
roar, Ruka heard when one of the higher servants broke the

first window. It echoed like a tiny symbol crash in her ears, immediately followed by three more when the other servants broke through as well.

Wolf was quivering. "I have to go to them."

Ruka grabbed his elbow. "You can't," she said. "You'll just get killed too."

"Have to," he whispered. "I'm sorry." He ripped his elbow from her grip and vaulted over the edge of the roof.

"What the—!" Michael yelled, jerking back from the edge. "That dude just jumped off the roof. Did you see that?"

Wolf landed on a dumpster, the impact denting the metal lid. Without pausing, he hopped off and raced down the street. Ruka watched him go, certain it was the last she'd ever see of him. And she'd only just started to like him. He flirted constantly, was annoying to the point where she wanted to hex him to death, but... If he died, Ruka knew she'd regret it forever.

"Oh, to hell with it," she said, and sprinted to the emergency stairs.

"Where are you going?" Huck call behind her. "Hey! Hey, I'm talking to you!"

"Just let her go," Wilson said.

Ruka took the steps two at a time, holding her skirts up so she wouldn't trip. The ladder was heavier than she thought, and it costed her a few precious minutes to lift it high enough to flick off the latch that kept it in place. She managed, though, and the second it hit the ground she was scrambling down.

"Ruka!" someone yelled and turned to see Nine at the top of the ladder.

"Stay here!" she yelled back. "If I don't make it, you need to tell the Mother what happened."

Regretting that she didn't have time to share her suspicions with Nine, Ruka hoped that the witch was smart enough to avoid any traps the Hunters had planned. Ruka knew the witch grew up on the streets, so she was no fool. Nine was cautious and could handle herself.

Halfway back to the church, Ruka decided that if she survived this, she would take an aerobics class. She took care of her body with light exercise and magic, but brisk walks didn't prepare her for a sprint across town. Her speed was pathetic compared to Wolf, but she didn't know if she should risk using magic to speed up, certain she'd need every bit once she arrived at the church. With only a block left to go, Ruka decided to trust that Wolf would keep himself alive until she got there.

By the time Ruka made it to the churchyard, Wolf was already fighting. His back hunched in an unnatural way and his arms were longer than any human should have, fingers drawn into deadly sharp tips. He moved like a hurricane of destruction; one moment he was in front of a clump of undead, and the next, flesh and fluids exploded into the air. Before the first chunks could even hit the ground he was gone, off to wreak havoc on the next bunch.

Gritting her teeth, Ruka grabbed a fistful of wood ash and gunpowder. She'd hoped to save the rest for the direct confrontation with the vampire, but she no longer afford to reserve power or materials. They needed to survive now.

The rune was the fasted she'd ever drawn, urgency forcing her to sketch the lines with lightening precision. Already, the undead had noticed her presence and broke off from the main group, ambling toward her with blank, milky eyes.

"Roken, vender shon, urzen," Ruka chanted, imbuing magic at the same time she drew the rune. It was an extremely dangerous way to cast, because if she made even the tiniest mistake, the magic would break the spell and explode in her face.

Forcing worries out of her head, Ruka concentrated on the rune. When she completed the last line, she was panting from the strain of holding the magic back.

Something groaned incredibly close. Looking up, Ruka found herself almost face to face with a zombie.

She threw out an arm to keep it off, but the thing twisted and sunk its teeth into her arm. She screamed, partly from the pain but mostly in fury, and fought to prevent the zombie from clamping down harder while maintaining control of her spell.

Her free hand fumbled to take the dagger from her chest bandolier, and Ruka stabbed it in the eye. The zombie stumbled backward, falling at her feet. Dead for good. Her left arm burned, bright red blood pouring from the bite, and she grimaced.

Ruka snagged a healing potion and, ripping out the cork with her teeth, chugged the whole thing. She made a face as it went down, the bitter taste almost worse than the pain from the bite. Within moments, however, the burning in her arm faded, and the bleeding stopped. It would be raw for a while, but when she twisted her wrist, was confident she'd still be able to use it. She sighed with relief, then looked at the zombie.

"Aberration," she spat at it, and gave it a kick. Irrationally, that made her feel better.

Ahead, Wolf was slowing down. He was still fast, but she could track his movements easier and he wasn't evading the muck explosions any more. Covered in gore from head to toe, he skipped backwards, trying to keep out of the zombie's clutches.

From inside the church, Ruka felt magic explode either Dusk or Wysteria trying to destroy the higher undead inside. There wasn't much time.

She held up her hand, the magic from the rune connecting to the power inside her.

"Burn," she whispered, and flung out her arm.

Fire and brimstone engulfed the church like the hell described in Dante's Inferno. The stench of meat gone bad turned into burnt hair and cooking fat as the zombies caught on fire, their skin melting and popping.

Wolf yelped and leapt backwards from the flames. He looked around, noticed her, and rushed to her side just in time for her knees to give out.

"Sorry," she said. "That took a lot out of me."

"What have you done?" he asked through a mutated jaw, looking back at the church in panic.

"Don't worry, I excluded you and the church from the spell," she murmured.

He smelled disgusting, but she didn't pull away.

"Don't worry," she said. "They'll get a little warm, but it won't harm them."

His shoulders sagged, and he pulled her in tighter. "Thank God. You're amazing," he said. Ruka brushed a clump of ash that had settled on his slightly arched nose, and when corners of his mouth curled up it her heart beat faster.

They'd dealt with all the undead outside, but Ruka was still worried. "It's not over yet," she told him, turning back to the church. "The higher servants are still inside."

"Hey! Wait up there!" someone called.

Ruka and Wolf turned to see the entire group of Hunters jogging toward them.

"Satan's hairy balls, would you look at this," Huck said, gazing at the inferno with astonishment and a bit of fear. "Guess we didn't have to come save you after all."

"Our people are still inside with the strong zombies," Wolf said.

Huck tugged at his moustache. "Right," he said. "You two look done in. We'll take it from here."

This was exactly the situation the Witch Mother had warned Ruka about, but nearly drained of magic and exhausted, she didn't have the energy to prevent him from stepping in for the final kill and saving the day.

Huck, Wilson and the two nameless Hunters made a four-man formation and wound their way through the dying flames. Quick bursts of bullets took care of zombies that hadn't burned to death, and within seconds, they reached the church entrance.

The double doors were still firmly shut, so Wilson pulled a small block of plaster from his vest. He pressed it onto the crack where the doors met, stuck a rod into it and backed away, spooling wire behind.

Huck hustled his men around the corner of the church. He checked to make sure everyone was there, and gave a signal to Wilson, who thumbed the trigger he was holding.

The church doors exploded in splinters and dust. The Hunters raced forward, guns up, and Ruka couldn't see anything more once they disappeared into the cloud of smoke and debris.

"Help me up," Ruka told Wolf. "We need to get in there. I don't trust the Hunters to kill those higher servants, and even if they do, I'm worried the Hunters might take advantage of the situation."

Wolf picked her right up, and it showed how tired he was that he grunted with the effort. Ruka was grateful and tried not to urge him to hurry. While Wolf stepped around bodies, Ruka squinted anxiously through the settling ash. After the constant barrage of undead cries, the crackle of dwindling fire and a few lone moans were almost disturbing.

From inside the church, a man screamed, and her pulse jumped. Guns burst into a constant rat-a-tat and then two more screams shattered the air before dying down into pathetic gurgles.

Four figures stepped from the church, and Ruka knew immediately they weren't Hunters. Wolf jerked to a stop, still holding Ruka, and she could feel his growl vibrating in his chest.

At first she thought the higher servants were mutants, deformed with lopsided shoulders, but as the air cleared she realized each one was holding a body draped over their shoulders. Three took off in a broken gait, the arms of their captives flopping awkwardly. She gasped when she recognized Wysteria's purple robes and Dusk's long, gray braid.

The fourth, however, noticed Ruka and Wolf and stopped. It twitched its head to one side.

Wolf snarled, and Ruka brought up her hand, fingertips visibly glowing with magic.

This undead's eyes somehow carried intelligence with their cloudy depths, and Ruka imagined it looked at them with delighted interest. It dropped the two Hunters it was carrying and took a step toward them.

Ruka summoned up every drop of magic she could spare, cold and shaky from the effort. Wolf put himself in front of her, snarling at the creature.

A loud boom hit her ears, and the servant's right arm disappeared into a misty spray.

From the church door, Huck stumbled out holding a shotgun. He'd taken a beating: blood dribbled down his face from a cut on his head, creating a red blot against his bandana and dripping down into his handlebar moustache.

"You killed my men," he mumbled. He had to grip the door's edge to keep from falling over.

The servant shrieked, not in pain but in anger. It picked up the Hunters it had dropped and put both over one shoulder with magically enhance strength, then loped off after the others.

Wolf set Ruka carefully on her feet and she stood trembling, her mind blank.

"Shoot them!" Huck hollered, his voice slurred. "Why aren't you shooting them, dammit!?"

"I'd risk hitting your men," she said, unwilling to confess that she barely had enough magic left for a single spell.

Huck punching the door. "Fuck!"

"Ruka!" someone yelled, and Ruka numbly turned to see Nine running toward them, her skirts held high. "What happened! Where are Wysteria and Dusk?"

"They're gone," Ruka said, swaying on her feet.

Nine reached them and gripped both Ruka's arms. "Where? Was it the vampire?"

Ruka nodded. "Yes. It just — its servants took them all."

"We'll get them back," Wolf said. "We will hunt that thing down and kill it so thoroughly it can never come back."

"Those motherfuckers," Huck said, drops of blood falling from his chin. "They took Archie and Doug, and killed Anderson and Stephan. Killed one of yours, too," he added, waving his hand vaguely at Wolf.

"I know," Wolf said. He was calm now, and sorrowful. "I felt Porkchop die."

"Wilson! Wilson, get your ass over here!" Huck called behind him, and a second figure appeared in the entrance, gripping the remnants of the door for support.

Huck was still shell-shocked, but the look in his eye was deadly.

"Buckle up, son," he said. "Because we are going to kill that blood-sucking, kid-touching, goat-fucking son of a bitch."

Ruka gritted her teeth. "Not if I kill it first."

THE MOMENT the four remaining members of their group were safely back inside the hotel, Wolf took Huck by the throat and slammed him hard enough against a wall to break it.

"What—" Huck gasped, scratching at Wolf's hand.

"Let him go, mutt," Wilson said, staring down a rifle aimed

at Wolf's head. "Let him go or I'll put a bullet through that brain of yours. Werewolf or not, your head can't grow back."

It seemed he'd forgotten about her, which was a mistake.

Ruka drew up a spark of magic and flicked it at Wilson with sour satisfaction. The Hunter grunted and his entire body went limp, then he dropped to his knees, the gun rattling on the ground. Three of the civilians cleared the room as fast as they could, but the kid Michael stopped just outside the door, peeking around the edge with wide eyes.

Nine swore but made no move to intervene and instead found a wall to put her back to. The witch's expression was calm, but Ruka could feel the magic just beneath the surface, ready to help. She was grateful for her sister's support, because this was about to get nasty.

"Be quiet and stay down," Ruka said. "I'm running short on time and patience, so I suggest you answer all of our questions."

Huck looked between the two of them uneasily, struggling to breathe. "Got it," he managed to get out. "I got it. Put me down."

Wolf opened his fingers, and the Hunter fell to the ground, coughing and rubbing his throat.

"What do you want to know?" he wheezed.

Ruka already knew the first question she wanted to ask. "How long have you known about the vampire?"

Huck glanced over at Wilson, who had eased himself to a place against the wall. "Not long," he said. "Just a bit longer than you."

Wolf crouched and peered at the Hunter with golden, glowing eyes. "You're lying," he said. He grabbed one of Huck's fingers before the Hunter could react and a muffled 'crack' sounded as it broke.

Huck screamed, spittle flying from his mouth, and he glared at Wolf with undisguised hatred.

"Thought you could slip that one under the radar, huh?" Wolf said pleasantly, a toothy grin spreading wide across his face.

"I — I can't tell you—" He screamed again as Wolf snapped another finger.

"Nope, wrong answer," Wolf told him.

The werewolf looked half-feral, and Ruka wondered if it was because he was seriously close to losing it, or if it was a show for the Hunters. He truly looked like he was ready to eat the Hunter, and Ruka remembered that Wolf had been hungry when they scouted on the roof. The undead took his food along with his packmates, which meant he hadn't eaten since the morning.

She reached behind her into a pouch and pulled out one of the spelled granola bars her apprentice made the day before. Moving to Wolf, she touched his back and resisted the urge to flinch back when he turned and growled at her.

His face blanked when he saw who it was, and he gave her an apologetic look.

"Let me take over for a minute," she said, and slipped him the granola bar. It wasn't much for a werewolf, but the magical enhancement gave extra calories. It was enough for now, and she'd make sure he ate more later. Wolf's hand clenched around the food and he retreated to a far corner.

Now that there was no immediate danger of a werewolf going crazy, Ruka eyed Huck. She wasn't fond of torture, but over forty years of being a witch had trained her to never shy away from what needed to be done, no matter how unpleasant. Then again, since it was looking like her suspicions were correct and the Hunters had lied to them the whole time, this might not be so unpleasant — well, at least not for her.

"I think we got off on the wrong foot," she said. "Why don't you tell us everything you know, and then we can work together to rescue our people."

Huck laughed without humor. "I see," he said. "Good cop, bad cop, right?"

She smiled sweetly. "Whatever gave you that idea?"

A twist of her fingers released the magic she'd prepared, and Huck's body tensed and jerked with what would feel like a powerful stun baton, a muffled scream emerging from clenched teeth. When the seizures settled, he looked up at her with teary, pain-filled eyes, snot dripping into his moustache.

"And I repeat: tell us everything you know. Neither of us will hesitate to torture or kill you, Hunter."

She leaned in and brought magic up to her eyes, making them glow with her inner power. "You see," she whispered into Huck's face, "we're not human."

With a swish of skirts, Nine crouched down as well. The other witch placed a hand on Ruka's shoulder in a very clear display of solidarity.

Huck's eyes flickered between the two angry, dangerous women, and swallowed.

"Fine," he said, sounding tired and defeated. "I'll tell you."

"Captain," Wilson started, but Huck waved him to be quiet.

"It's like you thought," Huck said. "We've known about the sucker for a while now."

"How long?"

He shifted uncomfortably. "Couple of months," he muttered.

Ruka prepared herself for the fact that the Hunter knew about the vampire before they called her to the farm, but months?

She heard the sound of a gun cocking a split second before Wolf slammed into Wilson. Scrambling backward, she saw Wolf gripping the Hunter scout's hand, a black pistol dangling from his grip. Wilson's face was red and screwed up in pain, while Wolf took the pistol delicately and tossed it behind him onto the floor.

"I had to," Wilson whimpered. "I had orders. It's not my fault."

Nine hissed at him like a cat. "Filthy Hunters," she said. She raised her hand and Wolf jumped back just in time to avoid a bolt of magic that crackled when it hit Wilson, causing the man's eyes to roll back in his head.

Ruka, angry at herself for letting her guard down, willed her heart to slow down. "Nine, watch him," she said, and the other witch took up a spot over Wilson, her fingertips sparking with magic.

Turning back to Huck, who clutched the hand with broken fingers to his chest.

"You said you knew about the vampire for months?" she said, her voice so quiet with restrained fury Wolf placed a hand on her arm. She shrugged it off. "How did you find it?"

Huck's gaze flicked to Wilson, and Ruka could see him still trying to figure out how to avoid telling the truth. She raised her hand again, causing Huck to cower.

"Okay, okay, okay!" he said. "We found it in a book! A book we got from some witch coven we broke up a few months back."

Ruka rocked back onto her heels, mind reeling. Of course! It all made sense. The raid on her sister coven, and the loss of many artifacts and tomes to the Hunters. One of them must have contained information about this vampire, and the Hunters thought it would be a good idea to dig it up.

"You mean to tell me," she said, struggling to keep her voice even, "that you found out about a vampire from a stolen book, and decided to wake it up to study it."

"We didn't wake it up," Huck said defensively. "The thing was dead. Or in some sort of hibernation. Least, that's what we heard. We took precautions - the book told us how - but the damn thing woke up anyway. The higher-ups think the witch working with us did it."

Wolf cocked his head and leaned forward. "You have a witch working with you?"

Ruka exchanged worried looks with Nine. Her first instinct was to vehemently deny that any witch would work with Hunters, but Huck's hard gaze suggested he wasn't lying. At this point, why would they make something up? If it was true, that was a whole other mess to deal with, but fortunately, one Ruka wouldn't be responsible.

Wilson groaned and his eyelids fluttered open. The moment his eyes focused, he saw Nine standing over him and flinched.

"Ya, we had a witch," Huck admitted, sneaking glances at Wilson. "How do you think we took out a whole coven? We made a deal: she'd give us a way in, and in return she'd get to study the vampire."

Ruka turned her back and buried her face into her hands, trusting Wolf to watch the Hunter. Shame and grief enveloped her, a whirlwind of thoughts and emotions shaking her to the core. She'd heard of witches who became disenchanted with their covens, even with magic. But she'd never, ever heard of a witch who betrayed her sisters, not in a way that resulted in their deaths. Especially not to Hunters. It was almost unthinkable.

Had the Witch Mother known? She had seemed desperate to make a deal with the Hunters for peace, and even though Ruka agreed it was a smart move for their coven, it was unlike the Mother to be so eager. Perhaps this was why.

"What happened to the witch?" Ruka asked, raising her head.

Huck shrugged. "Dunno. We rented an old milk farm and set up a lab. Had an entire team, including the witch, working there. A little over a week ago we lost contact, so we sent in Beta team to investigate. They didn't return. Not long after they went missing, reports started coming in of farmers disappearing in another area, so we sent in Alpha team to check that out. We hoped they weren't related, but..."

"The vampire killed them," Wolf said.

"Ya," Huck admitted. "We figured it was moving around, finding new victims, maybe a new place to live."

"Beta team, Alpha team," Nine said from her position over Wilson. "Which team are you boys?"

For the first time, Huck squirmed. "Delta team," he admitted. "We were the only team left, at least until we could get some reinforcements from out east."

Wonderful. No wonder the Hunter team seemed more like wannabe militia than efficient killers.

"Where was this lab of yours?" Ruka asked.

"Don't tell 'em, Captain," Wilson moaned, but Nine slapped his face and he shut up.

"About twenty miles south of there," Huck said, licking his lips nervously.

Ruka brought the map of the area to her mind and connected the dots. "Is the farm I investigated on the way to Rosedale from the lab?"

"Just about halfway between," Huck said.

She rubbed her forehead. "That makes sense, then. I supposed we should be grateful you built your lab in the middle of nowhere. If it were close to a city, we'd have a hard time finding it."

"It would be more cautious in the city," Wolf agreed. "It would hunt prostitutes, homeless, runaways. People no one would miss. But now that I think about it, why did it kill everyone here? Even though it's a small town, it would have known that an entire town going dark, plus missing Hunters would make all the supernaturals hunt it down."

Ruka's eyes widened. "That's why," she breathed in a flash of horrible insight.

Wolf looked confused.

"It wanted supernaturals to come for it," she explained, wishing to the Goddess she was wrong. But she knew she wasn't. "Because supernaturals provide so much more life force than a regular human could. It killed the entire town to gain enough power to deal with us, and now that we're here, it can regain much of the power it lost during its long hibernation.

"Once it's done here, it will move onto the city. It will take out the Hunters first because they're the least powerful threat. Then, once it's powerful enough, it will find and kill all the witches, werewolves and any other supernaturals it can get its hands on. This whole town was just an appetizer, and a carefully laid trap for us. And, Goddess help us, we walked right into it."

11

———

She was a fool.

She'd been so confident in her abilities, so convinced in her own superiority that she'd barely given a thought to the vampire's actions.

Nine and Ruka agreed to watch over the Hunters in shifts, with Ruka resting and meditating first. Ruka left and found an empty room, sitting on the floor and leaning her head back against the wall.

There were four and a half hours until nightfall. And with nightfall, the vampire would wake and become stronger, able to fully utilize its powers with the loss of the sun. If the Witch Mother sent help before night, they might make it. But the witches would still need to prepare, travel, and find the vampire. They'd still end up fighting in the dark where they were at a disadvantage.

Would it be better to protect the hotel as best she could and wait until help came? But if she did that, Dusk and Wysteria would surely be dead, and the vampire that much more powerful.

Was there no hope, then? No matter how Ruka looked at it,

death seemed inevitable. Death for her sisters, death for herself. Death for the remaining civilians, for the Hunters, for Wolf and his people.

So much death. Ruka felt like crying, but knew tears would do her no good. They wouldn't kill the vampire or bring back the dead.

A voice broke her reverie.

"Whatever you're thinking, it isn't that bad," Wolf said, easing to the ground beside her. He handed her a bottle of water. "Here. They have a bit of water up here."

Ruka took it. The cool water slid down her throat and she realized just how thirsty she'd been.

"Thank you," she said. "It helped."

"I thought it might," he said.

Remembering the granola bars in her bag, she pulled out the rest and handed them to Wolf.

"You were hungry again," she said.

"Always," Wolf admitted. "Half of it was with Denver, and the other half is still in the car. I thought this whole thing would take a few hours, and we'd be back home for dinner."

"Ya," she said, fiddling with her hands in her lap. "You're not the only one."

"You're beating yourself up over it," Wolf said.

She shrugged, not wanting to show how weak and stupid she was, and at the same time needing to talk to someone she could trust.

And she did trust him, she realized. With a few exceptions, he'd been cool-headed the whole time, and whenever she ran into trouble, he'd been there. He'd never challenged her, never doubted her. He went against every preconceived notion she had of werewolves. Even his werewolf brothers - his packmates - had been cooperative and efficient, instead of the wild, bestial idiots she'd expected.

"I don't know what to do," she admitted. "I — thought I had

things under control. Even when the vampire's servants took our people, I thought that we could get them back, and that we could kill it before my sisters arrived."

"We still can," he said.

She gave him a look. "I don't see how that's possible anymore. We might just be offering ourselves to the vampire as fuel to increase its power, and our reinforcements will have a harder time taking it down. But if we don't go, then my sisters back in the coven, and your packmates... they'll all die. The vampire has had enough humans, it will go for our people first. I don't know if I could live with myself, knowing that I hid in here like a coward while it drained every drop of blood from their bodies."

Wolf sighed and leaned his head back against the wall. "Ya, the same thought occurred to me," he said. "In the end, we'll have to make a decision though, and live with it. Or not. We might die, and in that case we won't care if we made the right decision."

A hint of a smile lifted her lips. "You have a unique outlook on life," she said. "Why are you so confident?"

"I don't need to be confident in myself," he said. "I just need to be confident in you. Whatever you decide, I'll follow."

She groaned and rubbed her face with her hands. "That isn't comforting," she said, and her voice dropped to barely a whisper. "What if I make the wrong decision?"

"Then I'll still back you up."

Ruka looked up into clear, honest brown eyes that reflected his trust. Trust she didn't feel like she deserved, and yet he was offering it.

"What if I decide that we need to try to save them?" she said slowly. "Even if it means we'll die."

"Then we'll die together," Wolf assured her, and it amazed her that he said it without the slightest hint of fear or hesitation. His warm hand covered hers, and she didn't pull away, grateful for his warmth and support.

"And if I choose to stay here and hold out for help?"

He gave a soft smile. "Then I'll stay by your side the entire time, and I'll join you and your sisters in taking the monster down."

This unwavering dedication should have increased her burden. It should have made her uncomfortable, but instead, somehow gave her confidence.

"All right," she said after a few minutes of deep thought. "In that case, we won't wait for help. We're going to save them."

Wolf laughed softly. "Thank God," he said. "I was worried for a minute you were going to make me a yellow-tailed coward."

She scowled and gave him a light slap on the shoulder. "Cheeky."

"Yes, Witchy, I certainly am," he replied cheerfully. Then he sighed. "Well, I guess we'd better tell the others. The Hunters won't be happy."

Wolf stood, and Ruka missed the warmth of his hand on hers.

He stretched. "Think they'll try to pull a fast one on us?"

She gave a predatory smile. "Oh, don't worry," she told him. "I have an idea about that."

Wolf helped her to her feet and Ruka eyed Huck and Wilson, who were whispering with their heads together. She checked to make sure she had enough magic for what she planned. The inferno spell had almost drained her, but she some magic had regenerated over the duration of their rest. She also had one last artifact left that she could drain the power from. It wasn't much, but every bit helped.

Nine, who had been meditating, opened her eyes when Ruka called her name softly. The Hunters wound down their hushed conversation and eyed the three supernaturals suspiciously.

"Wolf and I have decided to continue to pursue the vampire," Ruka told her sister in a low tone. She briefly outlined the conclusion she and Wolf had come to, as well as her suspicious about why the Hunters involved them in the first place.

By the end, Nine looked grave. "I see," she said. "You're right, our failure could have a grievous impact on the coven. But are you sure you still want to hunt it? Despite the risks?"

"Yes," Ruka said. "I understand this situation is more than what you expected when you agreed to come, but I still would like you by my side."

Nine gave a heavy sigh. "To be honest, I wondered if you would ask me or not."

"You expected this?" Ruka said.

"You aren't someone to give up."

Ruka nodded. "Will you join me then?"

The look in Nine's eyes was fierce and determined. "Yes, sister," she said. "I will join you."

A weight lifted off Ruka's chest, and she realized how worried she'd been that Nine would choose to stay behind. "Thank you. We'll begin our preparations shortly, but first I need your help."

She explained what she was going to do, and Nine's eyes widened.

"That's forbidden magic," the witch hissed. "If the Witch Mother ever finds out—"

"The Mother won't find out," Ruka said, "because I have no intention of telling her. Desperate times call for desperate measures."

"That's a slippery slope, Ruka," Nine warned.

"I understand, but considering the role they played in all of this, I'm not inclined to let them just run away and save themselves," Ruka said. She felt trepidation at the use of forbidden magic, but she'd made up her mind and would follow through, no matter the consequence.

Nine pressed her lips together, considering. "Fine," she said. "I'll do it. You'll owe me, though."

Ruka smiled. "That, my dear sister, is a given."

Wolf hung back while the two witches shared the contents of their pouches. They each grabbed a pinch of Nine's chamomile and mixed it with the remnants of Ruka's bone and ash mixture.

"This will be tricky without a rune," Nine whispered.

"Just do it as I told you," Ruka replied quietly. "If anything goes wrong, Wolf can kill them."

"Understood," Nine said, not at all bothered by the idea of killing the Hunters.

Ingredients in hand, both witches brought their magic to the surface, and when they were ready, approached Huck and Wilson, who had dark, mistrustful faces.

"What do you want now?" Huck asked, pulling his rifle up with his good hand.

Ruka didn't give him a chance to use it.

Almost in perfect synchronization, she and Nine threw the powder at their faces, and as the two men jerked back, coughing, the witches chanted.

"Urza, ruschta, bethda eh bethshi," they said as one.

By bone and blood, the power rises, my will against yours.

Ruka felt the spell weaving according to her words and will.

"Shu'un eihwaz, domina!"

Seal your fate, I command you!

The magic rose in power and the spell took hold just as Huck got the rifle braced against this shoulder.

"Stop!" Ruka commanded, and the Hunter froze, the tip of his gun wavering in the air.

While the Hunter leader fought, Wilson had flung himself

to the side, and his hasty scramble for the door ended by plowing face-first into the carpet.

"Neither of you may harm Wolf, Nine or myself, and you will stay here until I give further orders," Ruka said.

Huck, who had let his arm fall, looked pale. "What did you do to us?" he asked, his voice shaking.

"I've prevented you from abandoning the mess you put us and the entire town into."

"No," he breathed, turning grey as he realized what kind of magic she'd put on him. "You can't do this. Even I know this is black magic. You'll be thrown out of your coven, banned—"

"If that is my fate, then I'll accept it," Ruka told him. "But it's a problem for another day. Right here, right now, we will focus on killing the vampire and recovering our people."

"You're insane," Wilson told her from the floor where he was staunching a bloody nose. "You can't go against that thing alone."

"I know I can't do it alone," Ruka told them. "Which is why I've made sure you're coming with us."

"We need to know where it is first," Nine said with arms crossed. "Arabella said it was in an asylum, but none of us know about any asylum in the area."

"Um. I might know where..." a voice said.

The human Michael, who Ruka had forgotten about, was peeking around the door, his eyes as wide as saucers. While he seemed timid, he also was looking at Ruka and Nine with an awed and slightly thrilled expression.

The kid swallowed. "I mean, my friends and I figured something bogus was happening in the old abandoned military hospital, and like, he went to check but came back really scared. He said he saw zombies, and the zombies were bringing people there. Like, living people. He died later, though. But I think he was telling the truth."

"A military hospital," Ruka murmured, excitement fluttering in her stomach.

It fit. It would be a large building, abandoned, and explained the vision of an 'asylum' that Arabella saw.

She smiled grimly. "Tell me where."

THEY USED two precious hours to prepare. Though it made her shiver thinking of her sisters being held by the vampire, she knew that no matter how powerful it was, it could only absorb so much life force at a time.

The human Hunters she suspected were probably dead already since they contained little life force, but the witches and wolves would take longer for it to 'digest'. At most, it would have killed one of them, saving the others for later so that it wouldn't waste a drop of power. Ruka tried not to think about who it would have chosen as its first meal.

She made the Hunters rest. They claimed they couldn't sleep, but as soon as Ruka gave them a command to do so, it was lights out.

Wolf searched all three hotel floors and came back with a pillowcase stuffed with food. He needed the calories to replenish his energy and agreed to watch over the sleeping Hunters while he ate.

Ruka and Nine spent nearly the whole time in meditation, trying to speed up their magic recovery. Each had brought some precious stones they'd infused with their own magic beforehand, and Ruka used hers now to replenish herself.

When they only had two hours until dark, she rose from her meditation.

Ruka peered out the window toward the highway she could just barely see. "No reinforcements then," she said. "If our sisters were coming tonight, they'd be here already."

She expected it, but still felt anxiety creep up as she looked at just the five of them.

"Is everyone ready?" she asked.

Wilson gave a bitter laugh, and Huck glared. They would no doubt look for a chance to kill her, so she'd better be on her guard.

Everyone else was as ready as they were going to get. It was time.

Ruka stepped gingerly past a blob of what she thought used to be an arm. The street was empty again, only the smell and mess remained of the recent undead horde. She didn't know how many servants the vampire had left, but she was willing to bet it was a significant amount, maybe another thousand.

They followed one of the secondary highways out of town. Huck suggested they hot-wire a car. Ruka didn't want to give up their element of surprise, but after checking the sky, grudgingly agreed it would be a good idea.

Dark clouds gathered in the Northwest, a cool wind picking up and chilling the sweat on her skin. The air felt charged, smelling of ozone and rain. Ruka shivered. A storm was rolling in, and it couldn't have worse timing. Night would come sooner than expected, thunderclouds already creeping steadily toward the sun that hung low in the sky.

She stood back as Huck bashed open the front window and did something with wires under the steering wheel.

"Here goes," he said. When he tapped two wires together, the car started. He pulled a multi-bit screwdriver from a pocket on his leg and jammed it behind the top of the steering wheel to unlock it.

"Get in," she told the Hunters. "And I order you to not try to harm us." They'd used the bare minimum to cast the spell to make the Hunters obedient, and Ruka knew her orders would fade unless repeated.

"Well, that just takes all the fun out of things," Huck said with dark humor, seemingly resigned to his fate.

Ruka was surprised at how well he was taking his situation. More likely, he was trying to get her to let her guard down. Either way, it was better than Wilson, who kept glaring daggers at the back of her head.

The gravel road was full of potholes, and the car didn't have air conditioning. Ruka made Huck drive, sweating and gritting her teeth every time the car bounced enough to make them almost hit their heads. Despite the discomfort, driving was the right choice because it only took ten minutes to get to their destination.

When it came in sight, Ruka swallowed, overwhelmed by the sheer size.

The military hospital was an old three-story brick monstrosity. It must have been grandiose back in its day, when its masonry wasn't crumbling, when the whitewashed paint didn't flake off like leprous skin. The endless rows of windows lined up like soldiers must have sparkled in the sun when they were whole and clean, but now half were crusted with a yellow-brown film, and the other half held only shards of glass like broken teeth. The main entrance was still stately, but like an aged beauty, worn and drooping.

Everything about the place set off Ruka's instincts to run, and she wondered how they were going to find the vampire in such a massive sprawl.

Finding it wasn't their biggest problem at that moment, however. A horde of undead teemed in front of the entrance, shuffling and giving light moans.

"This is close enough," Wolf said.

Ruka agreed and ordered Huck to stop the car and turn it off.

"Sure thing," the Hunter said, and began fiddling under the dash. "Here's a little tip - not that you'll survive to use it - you turn it off by untwisting those two red wires. But then, I'm sure a high and mighty witch like you would never have to lower yourself to hot-wiring a car. Not when you can just order your slave to do it, am I right?"

Ruka struggled with the urge to smack the back of his head, but realized it was mostly nerves that made the childish idea seem so tempting. She got out of the car, with Wolf and Nine right behind. Huck and Wilson took their time, a watery form of rebellion.

The horde noticed them and were ambling over, their moans rising in volume and intensity. Ruka frowned when she realized there were four or five hundred of them.

"Can we go around?" she asked.

Wolf shook his head. "They'll just follow. Better to deal with them now rather than have them come behind and trap us."

"Do you think there will be more inside?" Nine asked.

"You can almost bet on it," Wolf said.

Huck joined her on the other side of Wolf. "So what's the plan then, oh powerful masters?" he asked with maximum sarcasm.

Ruka jutted her chin at the undead still a distance away. "We need to deal with them before we go in."

"Ya, I got that," the Hunter said. "What I wanna know is, how are we gonna do that? I'd guess you used a hefty chunk of magic earlier. So unless your sweet sister or wolf boy have a trick up their sleeves, we're fucked."

The left side of Nine's lip curled in disdain. "Be quiet unless you have something important to say," she commanded, and courtesy of the spell, Huck's mouth immediately snapped shut.

"Better," Nine said with satisfaction.

The sound of the engine startled them, revving to life behind them, and Ruka spun to see Wilson straighten up in the driver's seat. He turned the radio on and kept his eyes down, probably to avoid hearing or seeing either witch command him to stop. After shifting into reverse, he punched the pedal to the floor, and the car zipped backwards.

"What is he doing?" Wolf asked, more annoyed than worried.

"That sonofabitch is leaving me behind," Huck said with a disbelieving laugh, obviously considering this important enough to bypass the order to be silent.

Ruka pressed her lips together. "We don't have time for this."

Wolf tilted his head at her. "Want me to go get him?"

"Yes, please."

It took only a few enormous leaps for the werewolf to catch up to the car. After a very quick scuffle, Wolf brought back the runaway Hunter, dragging him by the collar. Wilson squirmed and swore, spittle flying from his mouth, but he couldn't loosen Wolf's grip.

"Now, hang on there," Huck started, "I'm as pissed off about this as you are, witch, but—"

"Captain Huck," Ruka interrupted. "Tell me. Did your team plan to use the witches and werewolves as a distraction while your team found the vampire on your own?"

Huck swallowed. She could see his mind working, trying to find a way out of this, but the spell demanded he answer truthfully.

"Ya," he admitted, the word sounding like it was dragged from his mouth.

"And did you expect us to be killed acting as distractions?"

He was pale now, but try as he might, the magic held him fast. "Not all of you," he said, staring with a stony face at Wilson, who had ceased struggling and pleaded at Huck with his eyes.

"I see," Ruka said. She then addressed Wilson. "You're quick to save your own skin at the expense of your allies. Tell me truthfully: were you leaving us behind to die?"

Wilson gritted his teeth, the spell forcing him to answer. "Yes."

"I've been suspecting you for some time now, but I want to hear it from your own mouth: did you sacrifice Ed and Stan to save yourself?"

All the blood drained from Wilson's face and his beady eyes flicked to Huck. "Yes," he groaned, unable to fight against her order to speak the truth.

She studied him, a mixture of revulsion and resignation swirling around in her gut.

Nine placed a hand on her shoulder, a show of silent support for what needed to be done.

"Should I?" Wolf asked, gesturing to Wilson.

"No," Ruka told him. "I'll do it."

She unsheathed her dagger, flecks of dried black blood still on the blade. Goddess, she didn't want to do this. But even if they kept the car, they couldn't just let him go; he'd never make it back to town. The undead were slow, but didn't need to rest, and would catch up to the Hunter in no time. Killing him now was the most practical, and in many ways humane, way to deal with him.

"No, please," Wilson begged, his deep-set eyes rolling frantically. "You're all crazy! This is a suicide run. You'll all die here, and if I stay I'll die too."

Ruka gazed down at him with a cold expression that showed no hint of her inner turmoil She didn't want to do this, but she didn't see any other way. "If we die," she said, "then I'll see you in the afterlife."

The undead were almost there, so Ruka wasted no more time. She took his hair in a firm grip and slashed the blade across his neck. Red sputtered from his neck as he tried to speak and poured down his chest like a river.

She let go of his hair and Wilson dropped to the ground, dead.

Ruka swallowed, trying to get rid of the acrid taste in her mouth, and plunged the dagger into his left ear, destroying the brain so that the vampire couldn't raise his body. She hated having to kill him, but at least could ensure the vampire wouldn't use him after death. Stepping on his neck, she pulled on the dagger with a sharp tug, freeing it.

"Why," Huck whispered, staring at his last comrade. "Why did you do that? He was under your spell. You could have just used your magic to make him—"

"Make him be less of a coward? Make him loyal?" Nine hissed. "It doesn't work like that. If we just stopped him from leaving and commanded him to stay with us, he would have found a way to stab us in the back sooner or later."

"But—"

"Our guests are here," Wolf warned them.

Ruka turned to see that the first undead had arrived. "We need to destroy these servants. Give Nine and I long enough to complete our spells," she commanded Huck.

The man's body pulled up his rifle in jerky motions. "Fuck!" he yelled. "If I survive this, I will personally hunt you down and put a bullet into your cold heart."

Nine was already drawing a rune in the rocky dirt with a stick. Ruka dug into the pouch she had readied and pulled out a fistful of powder, sprinkling it into the grooves.

They worked in tandem, Nine forming the lines for a hurried offensive rune laid overtop, a defensive one, and Ruka laying the ingredient base. They took a second to check their work, and each took a place inside.

"You're on defense," Ruka instructed her sister. "Make sure to grant sanctuary to Wolf and the Hunter."

Nine nodded, flicking her eyes to where Wolf and Huck struggled to keep the horde back. The Hunter was already bleeding in several places from bites and scratches, but he kept firing bullet after bullet into whatever undead brain was closest.

Wolf had half-transformed, the seams of his shirt ripped and barely hanging off a deformed, hairy torso. His legs were still human, but bent backwards like a canine. Despite his half-transformed body, every moment was powerful and carefully controlled, and he sent small packs of undead flying back with each swing of his claws.

"Hurry," Ruka said.

Nine licked her lips and steepled her fingers into a stabilizing formation.

Ruka monitored the undead as her sister muttered the chant for the defensive spell. She felt the magic streaming from Nine, curling along the lines they laid down, and snap into place.

"Come inside!" Ruka hollered.

The two men abandoned their opponents and ran back. Huck's eyes widened when he saw the blue barrier in place and tumbled into the safety of the circle right after Wolf.

12

———

olf stripped the remnants of clothes the moment he was safely inside. "Sorry," he said, standing stark naked and half-transformed.

Huck wiped his sweat nervously. "How long will this thing last?"

Nine's mouth pulled down, but she kept her concentration.

"Not long," Ruka replied for her. "But long enough. Wolf, this will take a lot out of me."

He nodded, ready to steady her should she need it.

The offensive rune only had six points, the most basic you could make, but it was the perfect size for a single witch. She took a place at the point facing the enemy and calmed her mind.

The horde arrived. They pushed in against the blue barrier, pounding at it with meaty fists. Behind them, the military hospital loomed frame by steel gray storm clouds.

The first raindrop hit Ruka in the face, but she barely felt it, so focused on bending and shaping her magic into place. When it was ready, she delicately pulled out her last marble and used a thin string of magic to crush it into fine dust.

The rain came down steadily now, and she allowed it to soak the mix of glass and sunshine in her palm. Pulling it close to her lips, she whispered her spell into it. The magic flooded in, tingling and burning.

Ruka thrust her palm to the sky like an offering, screaming the last word of her spell.

The storm responded.

A thick, blinding bolt of lightning fell to the earth like a shooting star. Ruka clapped her hands over her ears and squeezed her eyes just against the brilliant brightness. She crouched, shivering as the rain poured over her head, dragging her hair and skirts down with heavy water.

When she opened her eyes again, the blue of their barrier no longer existed. But neither did the undead.

Other than a few stragglers on the outskirts, who dragged themselves along with broken legs or missing arms, they had wiped the horde out.

Ruka's head spun and only Wolf's firm hold kept the ground from tilting up into her face.

"You okay?" Wolf hollered, and she flinched.

"I'm fine," she said, her throat raw and hoarse.

"What?"

She blinked and realized something dark was trickling out of the werewolf's ears.

He shook his head like a dog. "Sorry," he said. "Eardrums had to heal up. Are you okay?"

"Yes, I'm fine," she told him, and looked at the others.

Huck had collapsed on Nine, and Ruka gripped at him to pull him away, worried he'd done something to her sister. When Wolf pulled him off, however, she was relieved to see Nine was unharmed. The witch winced and shook her wrist gingerly, but it didn't look broken.

Huck, however, had not gotten so lucky. His ears, like Wolf, were bleeding, only he didn't have magical regenerative powers.

He'd protected Nine, Ruka suddenly realized. When the lightning struck, he'd thrown himself over her. Ruka didn't know whether it was instinct, a calculated response to win their trust, or he just didn't want the barrier to fall.

She pulled a health potion from her bandolier, leaving only two left. "Take this," she said, handing it to the Hunter.

He looked at her blankly until she mimed popping the cork and drinking it. Huck squinted at it suspiciously, but shrugged and tossed it down his throat.

He coughed and gagged. "What the hell is this? Poison?" he asked when he got his breath back.

"Healing potion," she replied.

"Could have fooled me," he muttered, and then realized he could hear again. "Huh. Tastes like shit, but it works."

Wolf and Nine had gotten to their feet and surveyed the ruins of bodies.

"Merciful Goddess," Nine whispered. "That was a hell of a spell."

"The storm helped," Ruka replied.

Nine eyed her. "You have anything left?"

"Some," Ruka told her. "Enough."

Ahead, Wolf tilted his head left to right as if listening for something. He suddenly froze, and just when Ruka was about to ask him what was wrong, bolted toward the hospital.

"Wolf!" Ruka yelled. "Where are you—"

"Children!" he called without slowing down. "I hear children!"

Ruka swore under her breath, and both Huck and Nine both sharpened their gazes.

"We need to help," Huck said, and for once Ruka agreed.

The three of them chased the werewolf who headed for a small, busted out basement window.

As she got closer, Ruka heard small voices. Most were

crying, but one child had stuck its fingertips above the windowsill and was calling for help.

Wolf fell to his knees from a run and gently grabbed the child's fingertips. "We're here," he said.

Ruka slipped and skidded to a stop beside Wolf, trying to peer down inside the window.

"How many are there?" she asked.

"Six," he replied.

Six children held captive in a basement. She didn't doubt they had to save them, but they couldn't take children along hunting the vampire. They needed to find a safe for them.

"Damn," Ruka muttered quietly, and only the twitch of Wolf's head showed that he heard. "Let's get them out."

Wolf pulled on the boy's arms, but the kid snatched his hand back.

"Are you a monster too?" the kid asked, his eyes suck on Wolf's distorted form.

Ruka cleared her throat and gently pushed the werewolf to one side. "No, we're not monsters," she said. "We're the good guys. This man looks strange, but I promise he's nice. He's very strong and can lift everyone out, but you need to take his hand, okay?"

"Wait," the kid said. "The other kids are too small to reach here."

Ruka could just barely see the little boy's face in what little light was left. He looked about ten years old, with shaggy blonde hair that fell in greasy clumps, and a face with traces of food around his mouth.

"What's your name, son?" Wolf asked, squeezing back beside Ruka.

"It's James, sir."

"James. That's a good, strong name. Can you lift the kids up, James?"

"No, sir. I can only reach this high because I'm standing on our water bucket."

Wolf turned back to Ruka.

"We need to get inside and lift them while someone pulls them out," he said. "I'm too big to fit in this window."

Ruka glanced back at Huck, who was larger than Wolf, and Nine, who's full bust and wide hips didn't look promising. Without a word, she shed her bandoliers and hip holsters.

Wolf politely looked away when she unbuttoned her skirt and pulled it down, leaving her only in her underwear and blouse.

"What are we gonna do with 'em?" Huck asked, peering past her worriedly.

"You're going to take them to the car, and get them out of here," Ruka said.

His body stiffened and for a second Ruka thought he disagreed, but when he tried to push himself through the window, she realized the spell was still in place and was forcing him to obey her order literally.

"No, wait," she said, and he stopped. "I'll go in to get them. Once they're all out, you can guide them to the car, and take them somewhere safe, far away from here."

Huck nodded in relief. "Would have done that anyway," he said, and there was a note of relief underneath the grouchiness.

Just as she stuck her feet inside the window, Wolf grabbed her arm. "Be careful," he said with worried eyes.

Ruka nodded, and he helped her shimmy in and gripped her hand until she could get her whole body in. She dropped to the floor, wincing in pain when she landed on her ankle wrong.

The first thing she noticed was the smell. If the stench of raw sewage at the hotel had been bad, this was simply abominable.

Ruka quickly tested it and was reassured that it wasn't

broken. She looked around, her eyes adjusted enough to get a better view of the room. In one corner was the obvious source of the smell, a bucket set up for the children to use as a toilet. Blankets, clothes, and food were strewn in random piles around the rest of the room, and empty food wrappers littered the ground.

She stood, hobbling on her bad ankle, and the group of children who had been slowly inching forward scurried backward again.

One, she noticed, stayed curled upon the ground, whimpering.

"She's sick," James said when he noticed Ruka looking. "I don't think she can move. I asked the zom — the bad guys for medicine, but they didn't give us any."

The boy was clearly trying to be brave for the younger children, and her heart twinged.

Ruka placed her hand on the girl's forehead, it burned with fever. The girl had yellow-brown stains down her legs, signs she hadn't been able to get to the makeshift toilet in time.

She went back to the window. "Nine, toss me one of my health potions," she called. "Wait, make that two."

Nine passed them to Wolf, who handed them to her. Ruka tucked one into her bra in case her ankle got worse and uncorked the second, pouring it down the little kid's throat.

The girl coughed and sputtered, but was too weak to resist, and soon Ruka got most of it down.

"I want my mommy," the girl replied in a watery voice, and then immediately broke into frightened sobs.

The boy hugged the little girl and pulled her to her feet. "Sshhh, it's okay," he said. "They're gonna help us get out."

"Sounds like she's better," Wolf said, and Ruka could hear the smile in his voice.

Ruka was relieved, but the child was making too much

noise. She kept herself low to the ground and reached out a hand. "Sweetheart, we need to get out of here before the bad guys come back, so I need you to be brave, okay?"

The girl stared at Ruka for a second, then took the offered hand with her tiny fingers. Ruka pulled the girl in gently and picked her up, lifting her to the window where Wolf waited.

"How come you don't have clothes?" the girl asked, and Ruka couldn't help but give a quiet laugh.

Leave it to kids to notice nudity in a life or death situation.

One by one, she lifted the children until the boy James was the only one left. She tried to lift him like she had the others, grunting from the effort, but he was too heavy and she was tired.

"Hold on," she said. "I'll crouch down and you can stand on my back."

A scraping sound from somewhere near inside the building made them both spin toward the door. She held her breath, ears straining.

At first there was nothing and Ruka thought she'd imagined it, until a moan echoed through the building, quickly followed by dozens of others.

"They're coming," James said, and his small body shook uncontrollably. "They come and grab a kid sometimes. They're gonna get us."

He'd been incredibly brave before, but now tears streamed down his face, leaving clean trails over dirty cheeks. More noise came from the hall: a background of many slow, shuffling footsteps, and a single pair of strong, sturdy ones.

Ruka crouched. "Climb on my back," she said. "Hurry."

The kid wasted no time and scrambled up. Even when he accidentally kicked her in the rib, Ruka didn't make a sound.

In the hallway just behind the door, single footsteps picked up speed, running toward the door.

She waited fretfully until his weight was lifted off her, and she could reach for Wolf.

The door to the room slammed open, and Ruka spun to see a higher undead servant standing in the doorway. Its milky eyes took in the empty room, the window, and Ruka pressed tightly against the wall, too terrified to move.

She stared at it. Her heart pounding so hard, but she couldn't breathe.

Then it roared and sprang at her faster than she thought possible.

Ruka shrieked and reached for the window, Wolf clamped around her wrists hard enough to bruise. He lifted her, but the servant grabbed her good foot. She kicked desperately with her feet and yelped when her sprained ankle connected.

Pain shot up her leg, and that pause was all the undead needed to get a better grip and rip her backwards with enough force to wrench her wrists from Wolf. She threw her hands out, but her head still hit the wall, stunning her hard enough that black sparks floated along the edge of her vision.

"No!" someone yelled and groggily realized it was Wolf. "Give her back! No!"

The yells turned into wild howls, and as the undead servant dragged her across the floor out of the room, Ruka had just enough clarity of thought to hope that the children and Nine got away before Wolf lost control.

THE HIGHER UNDEAD servant took her deeper into the hospital.

Ruka swam to full consciousness, and the moment she realized an undead gripped her arm on each side, she flew into a panicked struggle, even slamming a shot of raw magic into one servant, knocking it over. The moment she got to her feet to run, her ankle collapsed under her. She struggled up to her knees, but two more higher servants and a dozen regular zombies surrounded her.

She was trapped.

The lower undead lunged and snapped at her, their ragged nails scratching her skin and leaving burning red welts that oozed blood, but none of them put their teeth on her. The last slivers of sun peeked through dirty basement windows, but even though it wasn't fully dark, it seemed the vampire could still control its servants. She shivered when she realized it must want her alive and fresh.

Rather than expend all her energy in more futile attempts to escape, Ruka slowly raised trembling hands in surrender. She wished she had her tools and weapons with her, but she didn't regret helping the children get out. Wolf would make sure they got away safely. She knew it. Now she had to focus on what was to come.

Straightening her shoulders, Ruka let herself be pushed along by the undead, her head high as they lead her through the basement's long corridor, limping and stumbling over garbage, broken plaster and rusted chairs strewn along the path. At the end of the corridor, they guided her up a set of stairs and into an open courtyard.

It was still raining and sharp drops stung against her skin before running down her bare legs. She felt exposed without her skirts, her blouse barely covering her undergarments, and the moisture plastered the white fabric against her skin.

It was dark now. Not fully night, but the storm had extinguished almost all remaining hints of sun, and around her, undead stood like swaying statues, letting the rain and wind whip around them, washing congealed ichor to the ground.

Time seemed to slow as she walked among them, her escort forcefully clearing a path.

Lightning flashed, turning the bodies slick and glossy in its light, and Ruka saw hundreds upon hundreds of them packed together, the rain plastering hair to their skulls. Death and rot had erased much of the people they'd once been, but Ruka still saw a baseball hat here, a pink housecoat there, even one still clutching a broken dog leash that dangled above the ground.

In the very middle of the courtyard stood a small, two-story building. Ruka had no doubt in her mind that this was the vampire's lair. She would meet it for the first time in just moments, coming face to face with the monster who had slaughtered thousands of innocent people.

And yet, she didn't feel afraid.

Somewhere out there, Wolf was coming for her. She could feel it. If she died - when she died - she knew he would still come for her.

The thought made her heart clench.

The door to the building opened, and Ruka blinked against a glow of light. Yet she balked, unable to rid herself of the sense that, despite the light, the darkness inside was worse than the angry storm outside.

The higher servants pushed her forward and the moment she stepped inside, a sucking noise drew her attention to the far left. She slowly turned her head, fear returning in a rush and making her heart leapt to her throat.

The vampire had woken for the night. It sat on a heavy chair, like a king on his throne, surrounded by dozens of candles dripping wax onto the floor. Its body was so desiccated and warped by magic that Ruka couldn't tell if it had been male or female, and its skin was like gray paper stretched over sharp bones, completely devoid of hair. Even if it wasn't disgustingly ugly, a lasting sense of wrongness emanated from it.

Ruka shook as it lifted its head from the body of Porkchop and looked at her with eyes of endless black.

It was the incarnation of evil, and as they met eyes, Ruka had never felt such a sense of violation and revulsion. A smile spread deliberately across its face and it attacked the werewolf again, stabbing long, needle fangs into the neck of its prey, then sucked with such delight that Ruka emptied the remnants of her stomach. The creature seemed to take delight her misery, stopping to smack its lips and check to see if Ruka was still watching before drinking again.

She realized with horror that Porkchop was still alive, tears trailing down his round face, his gaze begging her. Not to save him; to kill him. The werewolf was in agony and wanted the release of death.

Ruka had to look away, overwhelmed by anguish and helplessness, and it was then she noticed the other bodies beside the throne. Her heart sank further when she recognized the last missing wolf, Benny, and her sisters Dusk and Wysteria. She mourned their deaths, until Wysteria's arm jerked, causing her to suck in a sharp breath.

Her eyes flew to the vampire in panic, but it hadn't noticed, still absorbed in its meal.

As Ruka's gaze returned to her sister, Wysteria twitched and rolled her eyes desperately, but it seemed she couldn't move beyond that. Both witches were missing their gear, destroying the hope that Ruka could construct an impromptu escape plan. All she had was the single health potion, still tucked safely under her breast, and her own wits.

It might not be enough to do anything, but Ruka would die fighting.

The vampire finished its meal and tossed the body aside like it weighed nothing, then wiped its mouth with more care and grace than Ruka expected from such a monster.

"Welcome," it said, and she shuddered at its raw, gravelly voice. "I've been expecting you. I am a gracious host, yes? Did you like the little surprises I left for you?"

Ruka refused to reply, or even look at it. There was nothing to say to this creature.

It twitched its head to the side, surveying her. "Little mortal, how many more will come?"

She still didn't answer, and it chattered its teeth at her in anger.

"The silent type," it hissed.

Then it laughed, sending sharp chills up Ruka's spine.

"Don't worry, don't worry," the vampire crooned. "You will be happy to tell me soon. You and your kind are nothing compared to my power."

She felt a spell rise from it, oily and disgusting. It came straight for her, and Ruka hastily summoned up what tattered fragments of power she had left. The two magics crashed together, and she gritted her teeth, struggling to hold her ground.

The vampire clacked its teeth together.

"I remember you. You are stronger than the others," it said, its voice grating like two stones rubbing against each other. "Good, good. Your blood will give me great power."

It raised its hand, and with a flick of its fingers something hit her from behind, slamming her to her knees and pushing her onto her belly. Concentration broken, the rancid magic circled around her and squeezed.

She hastily pulled her magic close to form a hard shell around the core of her being. It wouldn't hold, and Ruka knew she had only seconds before it took over completely, but suddenly the pressure stopped.

The vampire said something to its servants in a language Ruka didn't recognize. Mushy fingers grabbed her arms, Ruka panicked momentarily, but the undead servants were merely dragging her to her sisters, and Ruka stopped trying to struggle. For some reason, the vampire did not shatter the last resistance she'd placed. An ember of hope glowed in her chest. Maybe it didn't know.

The undead dumped her beside Wysteria, then gathered

around their master, groaning and petting it like obsessed attendants. Their gray, bloated hands caressed its shoulders, its knees and feet, and the vampire tilted its head back, preening with satisfaction as dead fingers slid over its body. The vampire made clucking noises at them like a human would to a pet.

Ruka eyed the appalling pageantry, then moved her head slowly and carefully until she could look at Wysteria. Her sister witch was still watching her, moisture gathered in her eyes.

"Can you move?"

Ruka mouthed the words instead of speaking them, and Wysteria's eyes widened. The witch pressed her lips together so hard they went white. She managed to twitch her shoulder and give Ruka a tiny nod.

"Dusk?" Ruka asked.

Wysteria rolled her eyes toward the older witch, who was lying with her back to them. "Don't know," she mouthed.

Ruka brought up a tiny tendril of magic to her fingers. Glancing back to the ghastly group of undead grooming the vampire, she eased out the tendril and extended it to Wysteria.

A thick coating of rancid magic coated the other witch. It fought Ruka when she tried to pierce it, and movement at the throne ceased. Ruka ceased immediately, her heart beating fast. The vampire stood up. Had it noticed? Was it going to kill her?

Instead of approaching, however, it glided across the room and left through the door Ruka came in, its servants trailing dutifully behind.

She let go of the breath she'd been holding, squeezing her eyes shut and saying a quick prayer of thanks to the Goddess.

Opening her eyes again, she sharpened control over her magic and pierced the spell around Wysteria. She wiggled it further in, and the instant she felt the hot, living power of Wysteria's core, withdrew to let her sister take over.

Wysteria's face screwed up in concentration and then sagged in relief. The witch quietly drew her arm up to her chest, a sure sign that she'd overcome the vampire's spell. She reached inside her shirt and drew out a necklace.

Ruka narrowed her eyes. It was a Virgin's Heart, a rare stone that contained powerful life magic. It was a tricky artifact: a witch on the verge of death could break it, and the stored magic would become invigorated, but it came with a cost felt later on.

Wysteria held it out with a shaky hand, offering it to Ruka. But Ruka knew the vampire's power. It wouldn't be enough.

Unless...

She gave a tiny shake of her head and flicked her eyes to indicate the vampire behind her. Wysteria's brows drew together, not understanding.

"It won't give me enough power," she whispered, "but it the life magic inside can destroy the vampire."

Wysteria bit her lip, thinking for a minute. "We'll need a rune," she whispered back. "I don't know any that would work."

"I do," Ruka said. "It's a high magic."

The other witch swallowed. "We'll need to provide the power for it, won't we?"

Ruka's eyes were hot with unshed tears. "Yes. We will."

They both knew what that meant. The spell would take every last drop of their magic, and that meant death. Even then, it might not be enough.

"Dusk," Wysteria said in a hoarse voice, but Ruka was already on it.

She slipped another thread of her magic toward the older witch, pushing past the spell that held Dusk captive. She was sweating by the time she made an opening.

Dusk stirred as her own magic fought to hold the gap in the vampire's spell, then stabilized. The old witch rolled over painfully.

"I heard," she whispered. "I will offer my magic and my life to destroy it."

Ruka reached out to each of her sisters, taking their hands in hers.

"We keep the balance," she whispered.

"We protect our sisters," they whispered back.

Outside, the undead stirred again, giving low moans that made Ruka clench in fear. The vampire was coming back.

13

They were running out of time.

Another body writhed and flopped beside them, and Ruka tensed until she realized it was the werewolf Benny, straining against the spell that held him. She crawled over on her elbows, keeping an eye on the door, until she could see his face. He looked angry and terrified by his helplessness, gold fading in and out of his eyes.

"I can try to free you," she whispered, "but it's coming back."

He stilled, trembling, and his eyes flicked toward the door the vampire left through.

"My sisters and I can kill it, but we need enough time to set up our spell. Can you buy us that time?"

She watched emotions ripple over him: terror, despair, and then finally acceptance. He'd heard everything the witches said and knew that helping them meant giving up all hope of escaping. To his credit, even though he trembled with fear, he jerked his chin in firm agreement.

Ruka was so, so tired. But she gritted her teeth and went through the whole process again, using her magic to create the tiniest break in the spell. Unlike her sisters, however, his wolf magic was wild and it pushed out of the gap until the evil magic stretched and popped like a balloon.

The undead outside shrieked and roared, responding to their master's realization his prey was escaping.

"Hurry!" Ruka yelled, pushing up to her hands and knees. Everything hurt and only adrenaline was holding her up now.

Her vision spun as she braced herself. They only had moments.

Her legs were already bare, so Ruka grabbed a broken flake of glass from the floor, making a deep slice in her leg. Blood poured from the wound and she gathered it into her palms, tracing a circle along the floor. Even if she had her materials, blood magic was immensely powerful, and even if they failed, it gave her satisfaction that the vampire would never have this for itself.

Dusk and Wysteria copied her, and she left them to draw the circle while she painted ancient symbols inside of it with numb, slick hands.

The door exploded inward and the first higher undead servant appeared with a roar. Ruka risked a quick glance and saw the werewolf tackled it down with enough force to break its legs. He reeled back immediately as more undead swarmed forward, slashing through dead flesh as hard as he could, but still undead poured through in an endless wave, and within seconds he was buried under a mountain of bodies, all clawing and biting for a taste of his flesh.

A higher servant crawled over the bodies on all fours, then straightened with a wheeze, staring at Ruka with hungry, evil eyes.

Ruka's breath came so fast she was almost hyperventilating. The rune was only half done, and she knew with a sinking heart that they would not make it.

Something crashed through the ceiling, and the higher

servant's shriek was cut off as it crumpled beneath a dark figure.

She knew it was him before she even saw him, a sense of familiarity that pushed against her heart.

Wolf. He'd come for her.

"Buy us time!" she screamed.

Without looking back, he threw himself at the undead, a flurry of teeth and claws, skin and fur that rapidly turned red.

Ruka kept half her attention on him and the encroaching horde, and half on the symbols, her breath shuddering. Wysteria and Dusk finished the parts they could help with, and waited with crossed legs inside the circle.

One more line, and the last symbol was finished. The gash in her legs had slowed to a thick trickling bleed, but she barely felt pain.

Dragging herself with bare, weak limbs, Ruka took her place in the center of the rune and desperately called for her magic.

It was pitifully small, a bare flicker of power that she knew was her last.

Please, Goddess, let it be enough, she prayed, and closed her eyes.

"Arzu, enaughola seithen, deirda," she chanted in a whisper that vibrated with power.

By life blood, seek out my enemy, the one who is dead.

"Ruschen, fehlette ud shon, huundah."

Send your power, burn with life, until all power is gone.

"Gremore, lune."

We offer from our bodies, everything.

Everything, Ruka thought, hot tears streaming down her cheeks.

The spell didn't want to form at first, and terror seized her, clouding her mind until she thought she'd faint. Then a warm rush of magic overwhelmed her as her sisters offered themselves to the rune. Their magic pooled together with hers and she grabbed it, shaping it into form, thin and delicate but growing stronger as it untied.

Wysteria left the necklace in the center for her. Ruka picked it up now, holding her concentration strong and trusting that Wolf would keep her alive long enough to finish the spell. Her very last work.

The magic built, trying to buck and spring from her grip. She felt transparent, like her existence was fading, but she held fast until the magic condensed and sharpened, coming to a point like a hunting dog.

She knew when the vampire entered the room. The entire horde seemed to shiver, a response to the power their master exuded. Ruka cracked open her eyes to see the creature in front of her and she gasped before she could help it. She sat trembling in the middle of the rune, gazing at the creature who stared down with eyes as black and deep as a bottomless chasm.

They couldn't win, she suddenly thought. All their efforts were futile. She'd die, and her sisters would die, and this being of pure evil would destroy her coven and everything she ever cared about.

Then something howled, and suddenly Wolf was between them. His back was bare and bloodied, and the sight of it snapped Ruka out of her stupor.

Gripping the necklace, she smashed the stone against the floor at the same time the vampire plunged its hand through Wolf's stomach, its hand coming out the other side glistening with blood.

Ruka's mouth opened in a silent scream as the spell tore through her. It felt like her soul was being ripped from her. Beside Ruka, Wysteria slumped to the ground, succumbing to the magic, and not long after Dusk gave Ruka a final surge of magic before falling to the floor in a heap. Now Ruka was alone.

The spell rose and sparked from her to the vampire, spearing it, and it shrieked in raw fury and pain.

Wolf wavered on his feet.

The vampire scuttled backward and retracted into itself like a leech sprinkled with salt, twitching and writhing as black smoke sizzling from its skin.

It was dying, Ruka realized with relief. Their lives would not be in vain.

All around, bodies fell in wet thuds, but she heard nothing but the sound of Wolf's knees hitting the floor. He slumped and fell onto his back just in front of her, a wet mess of blood and ripped flesh barely distinguishable from the undead who lay in messy heaps.

Then all was still.

There was nothing but the sound of Wolf's breathing, her own slowing pulse, and the rain.

The vampire was curled into a blackened husk, not even twitching.

It was over. They had won.

Ruka's vision darkened, and she wavered, barely able to keep herself sitting up. She knew without looking that her sisters were dead.

She also knew she would follow them soon.

Only a drop of magic remained inside her, and it wasn't even her own. It was the barest flicker left over from Wysteria's amulet, a flicker that would soon extinguish itself. And when it did, she would die with it. Her death didn't sadden her. She'd finished her work, and many, many lives would be saved thanks to the sacrifices of her and her sisters.

Ruka realized she was losing consciousness, and gathered the shattered remains of the necklace, gripping them between her fingers with enough strength to draw blood. The sudden pain cleared her mind for a moment.

Wolf still breathed, but in shaking wheezes that rattled.

Even his powerful werewolf magic had been completely used up, spent to buy her those few precious seconds. His soft brown hair was matted with blood, his face slashed and broken.

Ruka took out the vial of health potion, warm from her skin, and crawled to him. Every movement was agony, and blackness kept threatening to engulf her. Still she struggled forward, the few inches stretching into miles, until she reached him.

His breath came in stops and starts now, close to giving out, and Ruka's heart fluttered with alarm. No, she wouldn't let him die! There was no hope for her, but she would give the last of what she had to save him.

Ruka worked the potion's cork with numb fingers and wiggled it loose. Tipping the vial into Wolf's mouth, she blinked dazedly, waiting for it to take effect.

Nothing happened.

Please Goddess, Ruka prayed, feeling more sorrow than she had since she was a young girl and received news that her father was dead. *Please, I beg you. Let at least Wolf live.*

And then he coughed, and her heart calmed.

Wolf turned his face, and his beautiful gold eyes swam in her fading vision.

Good, she thought.

She smiled and closed her eyes.

14

———

Ruka's head was killing her. Her eyelids fluttered open, and a dark shadow loomed over her. A few blinks cleared her vision enough to see Wolf's anxious face only a foot from hers. He sagged in relief when she focused on him.

"You're awake," he said, and squeezed her hand in his.

"Wolf?" she said stupidly, her fuzzy brain unable to process what was happening. "Am I alive?"

"Ya," he said. "You're alive. I thought I'd lose—" his voice cracked, but took a steadying breath. "It was a real close call, but you're okay now. You're okay."

Scanning her surroundings, Ruka realized she was in the small infirmary of her Coven Hall. It was more of a bedroom, really, but with a wall of shelving fully stocked to heal magical and physical wounds. The bed was soft and clean, and her nose brought in a comforting smell of herbs.

In contrast, while Wolf had healed all his injuries, he looked gaunt and exhausted, his eyes rimmed red from lack of sleep.

"How did I survive—" she began, but the door to the infirmary creaked and Olivia burst into the room.

"Ruka! Oh my Goddess, you're awake!" Olivia's eyes were bright with unshed tears, her whole face lifting with joy.

"Quietly please, Olivia," Ruka said with a wince.

Her apprentice looked sheepish, and immediately lowered her voice. "Sorry, Ruka," she said. "I'm just really, really, really happy! You came back almost dead and have been out for two days."

Ruka's eyes widened. "Two days!?" she said, struggling to pull herself up into a sitting position.

Wolf hurriedly helped her, and fluffed the pillows before easing her back.

"Thank you," Ruka said, embarrassed yet grateful.

She felt like she'd been stomped on by a troll, everything sore and tired. Her ankle and head ached in particular, and when she moved she could feel the painful crust of a scab on her thigh that threatened to open, all wounds from fighting the vampire and its undead.

As if reading her mind, Wolf patted her hand sympathetically. "Your life energy was completely depleted, and they had to focus on giving you magical infusions to restore it."

"We had to save your soul before we could save your body," Olivia agreed, nodding and bustling around with the attitude of well-practiced nurse. "Health spells and potions don't mix with spiritual restoration techniques, you know."

Ruka huffed in amusement at her apprentice's lecture, fully aware that she herself had taught Olivia this.

"I see," she said. "Wait. If I was completely depleted of life energy, how did I survive?"

Her apprentice and Wolf exchanged a look, and Wolf looked uncomfortable.

"Uh.... So you remember when you were caught by the vampire, and I crashed through the ceiling?"

Ruka nodded. How could she forget?

The werewolf cleared his throat. "Well, I used some werewolf tricks to find where you were, and somehow..." He was incredibly nervous, which made Ruka nervous, but was funny somehow. "Er, it seems I formed a Bond with you."

A bond? Ruka was confused. A werewolf only formed Pack bonds with other wolves, there was no way he could have... Oh damn.

"You formed a Mate Bond with me?" She asked. When she focused, she realized now that she could feel it, a warm, fuzzy sense of Wolf's being that connected him to her.

"I'm sorry," he said, looking at her with his heart on his sleeve. "I didn't mean to. It saved your life, though, so I don't regret it."

This was a lot to take in. It explained how she had lived; the magical connection of a Mate Bond allowed a werewolf to share their thoughts, emotions and, it seemed, life force with their other half, so to speak. The downside was that a Bond was until death did you part. She had gone to find a vampire, and came back essentially married. It was almost more frightening than facing off hordes of undead.

Ruka suddenly realized that her goal becoming the next Witch Mother would be forever out of reach. Instead of feeling angry or dispirited, however, she felt an unexpected lightness and calm. Had she truly wanted to become Witch Mother, or had she simply wanted the promise of belonging that she hadn't felt since she was a little girl?

Wolf was still waiting for some reaction, tense as if expecting her to reject him, and she could feel his tentative hope, as well as the dread that hovered in the background.

She sighed. "Well, what's done is done," she said to him. "We can talk more later, you and I, and figure out how to move forward."

He swallowed, and a rush of warmth and careful gratitude

flooded from him to her. It was almost overwhelming, and Ruka needed to clear her head.

"Okay," she said, taking a breath. "I'd like a health potion, and I'd like to know what happened after I lost consciousness."

Olivia fetched the potion and gave it to Ruka, who grimaced at the taste. It was twice as potent as the potions she usually made, but twice as disgusting. Her sisters did good work.

"Well," Wolf said slowly, "when I woke up, you were just about dead, and only our Bond was keeping you alive. So I carried you back to town so that I could get a car and find help." He smiled. "Your witch sisters pulled through, though. They were already there, and when they saw you, they immediately started to do magicy stuff."

"Magicy stuff," she said, fighting to keep a straight face. "I see."

"I don't care what they did, as long as it worked," Wolf replied with a shrug. "Anyway, some of the witches headed for the hospital, and then Hunters arrived – Huck and the kids made it back just fine, by the way – and they got into some arguments about who was to blame for what, and who should get credit for what."

"Sounds delightful," Ruka said, grateful she'd been unconscious the whole time.

"Doesn't it, though?" came a voice from the door, making Ruka jump. The Witch Mother hobbled into the room, using a thick, knobby piece of wood as a cane.

"Your daughter greets the Mother," Ruka said, raising her hands to her forehead.

Olivia followed suit. "Um, I'll just wait outside," she said, and slipped out of the room.

The Mother looked at Wolf with disapproval. "Would you also care to excuse us?"

"I would not," he said, and leaned back in his chair with an easygoing stubbornness, still holding Ruka's hand.

Ruka hesitated, then said, "I don't mind him staying."

The old witch scowled, but moved on. "I've just come from a meeting with the Hunters – the last of several over the past two days – and you'll be pleased to hear that the peace treaty is going ahead, with all our conditions accepted. We also found several of the missing tomes that the Hunters pilfered from our sister covens, all squirreled away in the vampire's lair."

"That is a great relief," Ruka said. "I heard that Huck – the Hunter captain – survived, along with the human children. Nine was with them too. Is she well?"

Wolf's hand clenched around hers at the same time the Mother shook her head with a sad expression.

"I'm sorry, daughter, she did not."

Ruka closed her eyes a moment, grief welling up. She didn't know Nine very well before this mission, but had come to like and admire the witch. Her death was a painful, bitter loss.

"Rest assure, her death had meaning," the Mother assured her. "Nine, Arabella, Wysteria, Dusk: all of them sacrificed their lives for the welfare of the coven, and they will not be forgotten. The mission was a success, and we now have the Hunters exactly where we want them. Our coven will flourish and become stronger than ever."

The Mother sounded pleased, almost triumphant.

"You seem to think their deaths are an acceptable price to pay for this treaty," Ruka said, unable to help herself.

"Careful, daughter," the Mother said, her eyes glittering with warning.

Wolf's eyes turned hard and he lowered his chin, ready to defend Ruka.

"Oh, don't get your fur in a bunch," the Mother snapped. "We all mourn for our lost sisters, but I have dozens of other witches I am responsible for, and I need think of their futures too."

The old witch gave and irritated sigh and thumped her cane

on the floor in irritation. "I came to tell you the outcome of events, not get into an argument with you. We'll talk more when you're rested and thinking clear, but for now I have many matters that need my attention."

Opening the door the Mother waved Olivia back in. "Don't think me heartless, Ruka," the Mother said. "All lives return to the Goddess, you know this. A witch, especially one who wishes to become a coven leader, needs to use her head, not her heart. You'll understand that, given time"

Ruka would never understand that, and felt glad that she never would. "Goodbye, Mother," she said softly.

"So," Olivia said tentatively once the Mother left, "there are some wolves downstairs who need to talk to you. You know, since you haven't gone back home yet."

The girl was speaking to Wolf, of course, and Ruka wondered how much trouble he was in. His Alpha was likely upset with his extended absence.

Of course, it was then that Ruka heard the sound of irate voices and footsteps coming near. Wolf groaned and rubbed the back of his neck with his free hand.

"You can't be here, I said!" one of Ruka's sister witches said in the hallway beyond, and all at once, three witches and two werewolves appeared in the door. So much for getting rest.

Ruka's sisters appeared flustered and exasperated, and the wolves flashed their fangs and kept pulling themselves out of the witch's grasp. Ruka tensed and suffered a moment of panic when she couldn't draw up her magic.

"Sir," said one of the wolves, "we're—would you let go of me, witch!?" The werewolf freed his sleeve, then addressed Wolf again. "We're here to help with whatever you need. Do you have any orders for us?"

Orders? Ruka frowned at Wolf. "I thought you said you weren't the Alpha," she accused.

"I'm not," he said, looking sheepish. "I'm sorta just the Pack Second."

Her mind blanked. Pack Second was just as bad as an Alpha, maybe even worse.

"Well shit," Ruka said. She ignored the blatant open-mouthed shock on the faces of Olivia and the three other witches at her cussing.

"Settle into our safe houses and I'll contact you tonight," Wolf said with an easy authority.

The werewolves accepted orders without hesitation, and left with their witch escorts. Ruka let her head flop backward onto the pillows.

Something occurred to her, and she sat up again. "Wait. That means you're very dominant, doesn't it? Why did you let me order you around?"

Wolf leaned forward with melting eyes and nuzzled her neck, and Ruka felt her face heat up.

"Because you're you," he said.

Oh Goddess. She was in trouble.

"Is—is that so," she said, aware that Olivia was staring at the two of them with wide, scandalized eyes.

"Uh, I think I'll go now," the girl said.

Thank the Goddess for that. But then she stopped her apprentice. "One last thing. Did you give more thought to your witch name?"

The girl's face went from blushing to apprehensive.

"Um. I think—" she stammered. "I still think I want to go with Olive."

Ruka smiled. "Olive is a lovely choice."

Olivia's whole being transformed, practically beaming with joy. "Thank you, Ruka," she said.

They locked eyes, sharing a rare moment of understanding between master and apprentice that Ruka knew she would remember for the rest of her life. Then, with a final smile, Olivia left them alone.

"Witch name, huh?" Wolf said.

"Yes, her baptism is coming soon. I'll have to find someone to fill in for me since it'll take quite some time before I can use magic again."

Not only had she drained every drop of her magic, but she'd also used the Virgin's Heart. It was necessary, but the consequence was being unable to cast any magic for weeks, perhaps months.

Before all this happened, she would have been depressed and outraged by the setback, but right now, Ruka was simply thoughtful, and happy to be alive. Yes, a good rest was a good thing for her body, her magic, and her mind. It would give her time to think.

Everything still felt so unreal, like she was in another world. Or perhaps another life was more accurate. Life before the vampire, when she was powerful, respected and trying to keep her apprentice away from destructive influences. And now life after the vampire, when she was helpless, magic-less, and with the most un-werewolfy werewolf by her side, gently holding her hand. Life was so strange sometimes.

"You look tired," Wolf said. "Why don't you get comfortable and sleep some more?"

"I don't want to sleep," Ruka said. "I'll have nightmares."

He reached forward with a timid touch and brushed hair away from her face. "I promise I'll stay right here with you."

That sounded nice. How long had it been since someone protected her while she was sleeping?

"Fine then," she grumbled, and once again, Wolf helped her to get comfortable, arranging her pillows and tucking the covers around her.

"You know," she said, nervous for some reason, "maybe over the next few days we could take time to get to know one another. Now that we're not constantly in life or death situations."

Goddess, his smile was breathtaking.

"An excellent idea. Do you like coffee? I know a quiet place that makes a great cuppa joe and pie, and you can tell me all about yourself, including your name."

"You already know my name."

"Your real name," he said, and while he smiled, his eyes were dead serious.

Ruka sighed. "I left my human life a long time ago," she said, remembering those dark days after the war as an orphan, before the witches found her and took her in.

"I know a bit about why witches choose their own names, and even if I don't understand it, I do respect it. It's just... I want to get to know Ruka the woman, not Ruka the witch. I want to know all about your past, and share all of your future."

His hand was warm, his gaze warm. He was just too stubborn, and Ruka felt her remaining defenses crumbling. She remembered what Nine said in the church, about how the weak human she'd been had formed the powerful witch she'd become. Perhaps her humanity was not something to be ashamed of, but a necessary step to become who she was meant to be.

"Rebecca," she said finally. "My name is Rebecca."

Wolf smiled, and it was the softest, most tender smile she'd ever seen in her life.

"Nice to meet you, Rebecca," he said. "My name is Adam. Adam Waters."

ABOUT THE AUTHOR

EE Judd writes badass fantasy and science fiction. She's into reading (shocking!), video games and hippie stuff (crazy plant lady). Her energetic golden retriever make sure she moves enough to keep her soft little writer's body in shape.

She majored in Computer Programming in university, and then made good use of that education by deciding to write novels. In her spare time, she helps her husband run a dojo from their home, and knows enough jujitsu to get her in trouble (but not enough to get her out of trouble).

www.eejudd.com
@authoreejudd